THE PEARL NECKLACE

The incredible (mostly) true story behind the quest to solve the world's greatest modern-day treasure hunt

E. PAIRING

BALBOA.PRESS
A DIVISION OF HAY HOUSE

Copyright © 2023 E. Pairing.

All rights reserved. No part of this book may be used or reproduced by any means, graphic, electronic, or mechanical, including photocopying, recording, taping or by any information storage retrieval system without the written permission of the author except in the case of brief quotations embodied in critical articles and reviews.

Balboa Press books may be ordered through booksellers or by contacting:

Balboa Press
A Division of Hay House
1663 Liberty Drive
Bloomington, IN 47403
www.balboapress.com.au
AU TFN: 1 800 844 925 (Toll Free inside Australia)
AU Local: (02) 8310 7086 (+61 2 8310 7086 from outside Australia)

Because of the dynamic nature of the Internet, any web addresses or links contained in this book may have changed since publication and may no longer be valid. The views expressed in this work are solely those of the author and do not necessarily reflect the views of the publisher, and the publisher hereby disclaims any responsibility for them.

The author of this book does not dispense medical advice or prescribe the use of any technique as a form of treatment for physical, emotional, or medical problems without the advice of a physician, either directly or indirectly. The intent of the author is only to offer information of a general nature to help you in your quest for emotional and spiritual well-being. In the event you use any of the information in this book for yourself, which is your constitutional right, the author and the publisher assume no responsibility for your actions.

Any people depicted in stock imagery provided by Getty Images are models, and such images are being used for illustrative purposes only.
Certain stock imagery © Getty Images.

Print information available on the last page.

ISBN: 978-1-9822-9727-5 (sc)
ISBN: 978-1-9822-9728-2 (e)

Balboa Press rev. date: 05/04/2023

CONTENTS

Prologue vii

Chapter 1	As I Lay Dying	1
Chapter 2	Forrest	6
Chapter 3	The Thrill of the Chase	11
Chapter 4	Fennspeak	17
Chapter 5	Sin City	22
Chapter 6	Fiddlers Green	28
Chapter 7	Hunting the Snipe	37
Chapter 8	The Long Ride Home	44
Chapter 9	Closer	49
Chapter 10	WTF	58
Chapter 11	Full Circle	70
Chapter 12	Rest in Peace	74
Chapter 13	Salt & Pepper	84
Chapter 14	The Back Nine	91
Chapter 15	Jackson Hole	93
Chapter 16	White Xmas in Wyoming	96
Chapter 17	The Pearl Necklace	98
Chapter 18	Breakfast in America	105
Chapter 19	The Riddle	110
Chapter 20	Foray into Darkness	115
Chapter 21	The Last Supper	120
Chapter 22	The Chill of the Thrace	123
Chapter 23	Bloodlines	126
Chapter 24	Jackson	129
Chapter 25	The Peacemaker	134
Chapter 26	The End	138
Chapter 27	A long one	143
Chapter 28	Gone Alone	151
Chapter 29	Black Friday	156
Chapter 30	The Demosthenes Sequence	162

PROLOGUE

In everybody's life there are events that live long in the memory – the first kiss or intimacy, shooting that first gun, driving your first car, moving in together, getting married, having children. Then there are other random events that happen by chance but are equally life defining – the car accident where you lost the sight in your right eye, the guy you met at the Xmas BBQ that became your business partner, the time you lost $2000 at the casino and had no money for groceries until the next payday. For me, 23rd June 2017 was one such occasion.

It was the day after another life defining event. On the 22nd of June 2017 I had suffered a massive heart attack that almost took my life. The next day, after life-saving surgery, while convalescing in the local hospitals cardiac ward, I stuck up a conversation with Bob, the patient in the next bed. He bemoaned the fact he was 67 and had achieved nothing of real consequence in his life. He was determined to correct that imbalance the moment he was released from hospital. It was at this time he introduced me to the legend that is Forrest Fenn. This proved to be an event that would dominate my life for the next 5 years, and lead to the writing of this book.

Forrest Fenn was an octogenarian living in New Mexico. After living a colourful life, servicing time in Vietnam as a fighter pilot, and later running an exclusive art dealership in Santa Fe, he had decided to create a treasure hunt to get people back out into the great outdoors. For the last 8 years, thousands of people had been searching for a chest containing over a million dollars' worth of gold and precious jewels he had hidden somewhere in the Rocky Mountains. He had written a 24-line poem that held the secrets to the treasure's location.

Being a keen cryptic crossword guy and armchair puzzle solver, I was hooked. The next five years have been spent unravelling the multitude of clues that make up the Chase. It has been a wild ride of excitement and intrigue. On the surface, and just below, the chase invokes vivid memories of childhood stories of cowboys and Indians, pirates and buried treasure chests, secret societies, and machine gun toting gangsters. However, deeper down, the truth behind the chase becomes darker, and some might say, more sordid. At its inner most core, the solutions become more personal, and scarcely believable.

In 2020 the treasure was allegedly found. This book sheds new light on that event and brings into question the credibility of the purported discovery. It also raises an important question – was the discovery an orchestrated cover-up? Here for the first time is the truth that lies beneath the fabrication, falsehoods, and downright lies that surround the chase. As is so often said, the truth really is stranger than fiction.

CHAPTER 1

AS I LAY DYING

Gentle murmuring and the shuffle of feet led me to open my eyes to the morning light that floated in through the east-facing sixth floor windows. Five white lab coats were gathered around the end of my hospital bed. The lead coat towered above the other coats on either side of him. He was unusually tall, maybe 6 foot four, and of skinny build with very dark skin. In his left arm he cradled a clipboard, and in his right hand a pen, as if ready to write something down at any second.

He stared at me through his horn-rimmed glasses for a good 30 seconds, while peeking down at the clipboard every now and again.

"Mr. Pairing," he proclaimed in a loud and confident manner, "You're a very lucky man!"

The other white coats nodded in silent agreement. I gazed past the medical team at my three cardiac roommates. They were all listening intently from their beds, while pretending to be doing other things.

"A partial blockage of the lower left descending anterior artery leading to acute myocardial infarction".

The nodding of the other coats was more pronounced this time, as they all clearly understood what the head coat was talking about.

"Known commonly in medical circles as the widow-maker." He paused for effect, glancing to either side to view the reaction of the other coats.

"A major heart event that only 20% of victims survive if it happens outside hospital walls. Very lucky indeed! How do you feel?"

E. Pairing

"Lucky I guess," I offered up unconvincingly, while glancing down at my right arm. It was bruised black from wrist to elbow. A clear plastic collar was tightly clamped around the wrist to stop blood spurting from the vein the surgeon had pierced to thread a tube up my arm and across into my heart the previous day.

The operation had been planned to take 20 minutes under local anaesthetic. When I had arrived at surgery, beds were lined up along the corridor to the theatre like planes at LAX airport. My time slot was 4:20pm. I had been inserted into the line-up due to my arrival in an ambulance a couple of hours earlier, causing one bed carrying an elective surgery patient to be sent back to the ward until tomorrow.

Oddly close relatives were allowed into the corridor, and my family, who had rushed to the hospital on news of my heart attack were now crowded around the bed. It was reminiscent of kinsfolk huddled around the coffin at a funeral home, both strangely comforting and reassuring.

Right on 4:20pm a bed burst out through the theatre doors on its way back to the ward. An orderly appeared from nowhere and began pushing my bed through the still moving doors.

A surge of nervous anxiety came upon me as it was suddenly all to obvious that it was my turn up to the plate. The bright lights and whiteness of the room were overwhelming.

Despite the critical nature of the surgery, I was able to sit there wide awake watching the operation on an overhead monitor. The administering of local anaesthetic and the insertion of a lure into my wrist was relatively painless, however the same couldn't be said for the threading of the tube up my arm and into my heart.

Once this tube was in place, a minute piece of metal gauze tube was then fed up the tube to the site of the blockage. Unfortunately, this first stent was too small and didn't fit snugly into the blockage site.

"Shit," the young surgeon proclaimed loudly. "Get me a 14A," he barked at the even younger nurse.

She scurried off into a room adjoining the theatre, while the surgeon and his attendant made small talk about cancelling the next operation as it was now quarter to five and wanting to be at the casino by 6 o'clock.

The nurse returned with a small package. The surgeon immediately torn it open and extracted the new gauze tube with a pair of tweezers. With the precision of a B-grade mechanic he managed to manoeuvre the stent up the tube and into position. "Hallelujah," he proclaimed as he fitted the clear plastic bracelet, "Crown Plaza here I come."

After a number of post-operative checks I was shunted back to the ward to be reunited with the elective patient who got bumped due to my elevation into the queue, and two other elderly gents who had also undergone heart surgery that afternoon.

As my bed was pushed into position, my family trooped in and gathered around it. This time the mood was more buoyant than in the corridor outside the surgical theatre. An oxygen mask was fitted to assist my breathing. It meant the conversation went back and forward across the bed with little to no input from myself. My wife from my second marriage Heather did her best to keep a lid on the four teenage children who invariably got out-of-control when together. We were an unusual, blended family, made up of Colt, my 24-year-old son from my first marriage, and his full sister Briar-Rose, his step sister Lexie, and his half-sister Aura. As the decibel level of the conversation grew, the weirdest scene evolved. Even though the banter was becoming quite raucous, it was as if the room had fallen silent. I gazed beyond the immediate group surrounding the bed, over into the far corner of the room. There, the compression bracelet had popped open on 75-year-old Billy's wrist and blood was spurting from his arm like a very thin but forceful fountain. It was creating a Jackson Pollock-like painting on the ceiling, walls and curtains, and a large pool on the floor. I waved my one good arm about wildly to attract the groups attention to the life-threatening drama evolving behind their backs. Heather was the first to react. Grabbing a towel off the end of the bed she bounded across the room. Plunging the towel over the geyser emanating from Billy Bleed Out's wrist she pushed down hard in an effort to stem the blood flow. One of the kids grabbed the emergency buzzer and pushed it to summons the nursing staff. Over the next few minutes all hell broke loose as medical staff came running from all directions. Amidst the mayhem they managed to refit the bracelet to his wrist and prevent him bleeding out completely onto the floor and surrounding furnishings.

With the excitement over for the day, the crowd slowly dissipated eventually leaving just myself and the three old geezers, Bobby Bumped-bed, Billy Bleed-out, and Bryan Belcher alone in the room.

The night was surprisingly restful, interrupted only by the 4 hourly checks by the nurses making sure our vital signs were as they should be.

E. Pairing

It was about 8 o'clock' next morning when the white coat entourage made their appearance. After telling me how lucky I was to be alive, I was informed I would be staying another day, and due to that day being a Friday I would be kept in over the weekend and released on Monday morning, all going well. That said, they thankfully moved on to bother Bobby Bumped Bed in the next cubicle. They wished him all the best for his procedure that day before moving across the room to Billy Bleed Out. The curtains were pulled around his bed as if to afford more privacy, even though the conversation was no less clear with them closed. The doctor and his entourage discussed the unfortunate events of the previous day and the reasons for the failure of the plastic cuff to stay intact. They downplayed the fact that over half of his blood had ended up on the floor around his bed, and wished him all the best for a speedy recovery.

After finally finishing with Bryan Belcher in the bed directly opposite mine, the white coat brigade departed leaving the four old-timers in peace.

A long period of quiet ensued as we lay in our beds soaking up the early morning sun. BBO was the first to break the silence.

"Twenty percent chance of survival Earl. That must feel pretty good."

"It does mate. It really does," I replied.

"Well, what are you going to do with the rest of it then?" BBB chipped in.

"Yeah, you've been given this final chance, like an extra bonus. Surely you'll use it to do something special," added BB enthusiastically.

"Like what," I responded lamely.

"You know, bucket list stuff. Skydiving and shit."

"All that crap doesn't do it for me," I responded. "I'd prefer to do something exciting with the family."

"What about searching for hidden treasure?" announced BB.

At last, something that piqued my interest. "Hasn't it all been found?"

"Not at all, mate. There's plenty still out there. Oak Island, The Golden Owl, The Beale Cyphers. Surely you must have heard of Forrest Fenn's treasure."

"Never heard of any of them, Bryan, but would be interested to know where to look," I answered, trying to keep the flame alive.

"It's all on-line, mate," BB informed me, reaching for his laptop on the bedside table. "Here, I'll bring it up for you."

Putting on his glasses, he began banging away on his keyboard like a mad pianist. "Ah, he's a good one," he announced, just as one of the nurses strode into the room. "Hey, gorgeous, can you hand this to Earl please."

"Anything for you Bryan," the nurse winked, transporting the computer across the room, and placing it gently on my stomach.

I gazed down, and there on the screen was the most beautiful sight, a treasure chest crammed full of gold coins and nuggets. It was love at first sight. I knew I was hooked.

CHAPTER 2

FORREST

With my appetite whetted, I texted Heather and asked for her to bring my laptop from home when she visited later in the day. She was happy to see I was alert and still amongst the living.

In the time until she arrived I discussed with BB his theories on where the treasure was hidden. It was one of those situations where you are sure the person is way off target and are happy not to tell them that.

Right on 4 o'clock Heather arrived, together with a group of my football mates who had heard of my misfortune. It was great to see them, and they lifted my spirits immensely. We recalled memorable moments from trips away and games we had enjoyed, but eventually I found myself yearning for them to leave. No sooner than they were out the door, I was booting up my computer.

A quick search on-line of the greatest modern day treasure hunts revealed this topic is indeed dominated by one, the famous Fenn treasure hunt. Reading about it for the first time was one of those situations when you realise it is a chance meeting or event that is going to change your life. At the time you think for the better but there are niggling fears that maybe that's not the case. I remember I had experienced a similar feeling when I first smoked marijuana in the back of Mark Smith's car in high school. That didn't work out too well. I hoped this would be different.

The treasure hunt was created by an ex-Vietnam veteran Forrest Fenn, who at the age of 58, was diagnosed with kidney cancer. He was given a 15% chance of surviving. Realising his mortality, he looked on-line for his father's name, a man he had looked up to all his life. His father had been a headmaster, a fine educator, and an upstanding member of the local community. Fenn's on-line search uncovered only one fact about his father. That he was buried in Hillcrest Cemetery in Row 4, Block 23.

Determined to leave a legacy more profound than that of his father, Fenn decided to create a treasure hunt that would get people off their couches and out into the great outdoors. After beating cancer, he spent 15 years compiling the hunt, then at the age of 80, in the year 2010, made the defining decision to put the treasure hunt into play. He took the treasure he had compiled over a long period, placed it in a magnificent 10-inch by 10-inch chest, left his home in Santa Fe, and drove to the location he had decided would be the resting place for the chest.

After depositing the chest, he then published a book The Thrill of the Chase. Within the book he presented a 24-line poem, amongst other tales about his colourful life. He then promoted it widely. If you could correctly interpret the poem and solve its clues, you would be directed to the chest, with its $1 million dollars' worth of gold and treasure. He provided other pointers, dictating the chest was hidden in the Rockies somewhere within 4 states, being New Mexico, Colorado, Wyoming, or Montana.

I was now reading this in my hospital bed in 2017. Eight years after its inception the treasure was still undiscovered. By now Fenn had published a further two books, Too Far to Walk, and Once Upon a While, to provide further stories about his life, and most likely more clues as to the site of the treasure. Reputedly over 300,000 people were searching for the treasure.

My overwhelming thought was, how hard could this be! How many clues could you possibly hide in a 24-line poem? I felt energised for the first time in months.

The poem was readily available on-line. I found the most presentable copy and saved it to file. I then went to Amazon to secure a copy of "The Thrill of the Chase". It was easy to find but the price was steep - $155. I ordered it immediately. What was $155 when we were going to find $1M worth of treasure. That was $1M in 2010 I thought. A quick search revealed it was now valued at well over $2M.

While I waited for the book to arrive, it was down to business. Back at home from the hospital and off work for the next two weeks, I began converting the sports room in the house into a war room complete with map desk and pinboards. Large bookcases, a globe of the world, a stuffed eagle, and comfortable leather armchairs completed the fit out giving the room the desired ambience. National Treasure and the Indiana Jones series were all-time favourite movies, and what was a treasure hunter without his self-styled study.

Rather than try and solve the poem myself, I immediately went on line to survey other searchers views on the poem. Probably not the greatest strategy given no one had found the treasure, but at least it would flush out the prevailing theories regarding the Chase. It proved to be a good move as it gave an insightful view into the Fenn Treasure Hunt ecosystem.

Prominent in this landscape was a site run by a good friend of Fenn's, Dal Nietzel. It was a compilation of scrapbooks, mainly published by Fenn. Every so often, maybe weekly, or monthly, Fenn would send Neitzel a scrapbook, usually an anecdotal story, that would be then published on the site. By 2018 there were over 200 scrapbooks on the site. Once the new story was released there would be a rush of postings to the site from the faithful hordes following the Chase. Interestingly, all new posts would sit in a pending state until released to the site by Neitzel. In this way the site was heavily moderated. All posts were vetted for their suitability to be published.

There were numerous other sites offering possible solutions to the predominant clues within the poem. Like any other on-line communities, it was dominated by a select few self -appointed experts. They all had their particular reasons for being there. They had inspiring nicknames, and their followers hung on their every word.

Over the 8 years from 2010 until 2018 Fenn published a plethora of stories, primarily about himself and his life via a wide array of media. He came across as a modest, self-effacing man who had been a larger-than-life character in a long and colourful life. The stories told a tale of a boy, Forest Burk Fenn, born in Temple, Texas on August 22, 1930, to William Marven Fenn, a teacher at the local school, and his wife, Lillie Gay Simpson. As he grew up, Forrest struggled academically, finding his enjoyment with his friends outside of the classroom. Each summer the family would make the long journey from Temple to Yellowstone for the summer break. These were times Forrest loved immensely, leading to many of the tales Forest would tell in his later life. In his teenage years, Forrest developed an interest in cars and girls, buying a Plymouth Tudor he affectionally nicknamed The Bullet, and meeting the love of his life, Peggy-Jean Proctor.

Upon leaving school, without graduating, Forrest followed his mates to military college despite not being enrolled. He attended classes and other events until his cover was blown and he had to leave. During his time at the college Forrest realised his future was in the military and he enrolled into the air force. He trained as a fighter pilot travelling back home at weekends to maintain his relationship with Peggy Jean.

After graduating flight school, Forrest married Peggy Jean on December 27, 1953. They briefly lived on the coast at Mexico Beach, Texas, before being stationed in Lubbock. They had two daughters, Zoey and Kelly, before Forrest was posted to Vietnam in late 1967. During his year-long tour-of-duty he flew 326 missions, returning safely 324 times. On the other two missions, he ejected from his fighter jet into the jungles of Vietnam. These events had a profound effect on him, and the stories about these episodes feature prominently in his books.

Forrest returned home safely from Vietnam at Xmas time 1968, to be reunited with Peggy Jean and his two daughters. Following this joyous event, he continued in the services for a number of years.

In 1972, the Fenn's made the difficult decision to relocate to Sante Fe. Although knowing little about art they opened an art gallery featuring Native American works and artifacts. Despite their lack of experience, the gallery flourished and the Fenn's built a prominent and profitable business. This allowed them the opportunity to fraternise with the rich and famous. Actors and actresses, artists, politicians, influencers, and other famous people all frequented the gallery, and became clients and friends to the Fenn's. The time spent with these individuals provided more stories for the books Forrest would write later in relation to the Chase.

During his time in Santa Fe, Forrest bought a large pueblo in Taos named San Lazaro. He spent many of his weekends at the pueblo excavating the ancient ruins. Many Spanish artifacts were recovered in the course of the excavations. In 2009 his activities came under the scrutiny of the FBI. They executed a search warrant at this Santa Fe home and confiscated some of the items in his possession. No charges were pressed in relation to the items, however two other people involved in the wider investigation by the FBI committed suicide. This had a deep effect on Fenn who blamed the FBI for their deaths.

E. Pairing

By 2009 Fenn had largely completed the treasure hunt that was to be his opus magnus. In 2010 at the age of 80 he decided to push the button and put The Chase into play. It was to become the dominant feature of his life for the next ten years. The treasure he had hidden somewhere in the Rockies was made up of items he had gathered over a lifetime of collecting. Unknown to most who sought to find the treasure, each item had a special significance to the hunt. The golden nuggets the size of hens' eggs, golden eagles and double eagles in their hundreds, precious stones scattered in amongst them, a silver bracelet set with 22 turquoise beads that was very dear to Forrest, an antique gold dragon bracelet encrusted with 254 rubies, emeralds, sapphires, and many small diamonds, a 17th century Spanish gold ring with a large emerald feature, and an ancient necklace from Columbia with 39 animal fetishes carved from crystal, carnelian, jade, and other exotic stones. In addition to this there was two Chinese mirrors of polished gold, and small golden frog, and a 20,000-word autobiography sealed in a glass jar.

Fittingly the treasure was contained in a beautiful 10-inch by 10-inch bronze Romanesque chest emblazoned with pictures of scantily clad figures scaling ladders up the sides of a castle.

It was a spectacular treasure trove that would raise the heart rate and frequent the dreams of every prospective hunter to be drawn into its heady vortex.

CHAPTER 3

THE THRILL OF THE CHASE

It took several weeks after ordering The Thrill Of The Chase on-line for it to turn up in the letter box. By the time it did, I was back into the grind of 10-hour days at the factory. Its arrival was a fillip for me and the small crew that had been assembled for this life-changing adventure. The team had been gathered through a straight forward process. Those who scoffed at the authenticity of the Chase and the existence of the treasure were banished. Lead protagonist in this area was my wife Heather. From day one she was adamant the whole thing was a hoax. Who in their right mind would deposit $1M of treasure into the wilderness for a stranger to find? She took every opportunity to decry the chase and downplay the treasure's very existence.

Chief supporter was my 22-year-old daughter Briar-Rose. Recently burdened with a $450,000 mortgage there was 450,000 reasons for her to be a believer. Her long-time partner Tyler was along for the ride, as they were like Siamese twins, joined at the hip and had been since high school. He also had 450,000 reasons to belief. Completing the team was Colt, my 27-year-old son who you met at the hospital. He was young, intelligent, and adventurous. His main shortcoming was his inability to say no to people. There were two other wishful participants, but their age, parentage, and other commitments to school and sport precluded them from joining the team. An attempt was made to recruit some of my middle-aged friends to the team, but they all had trouble explaining it to their spouses.

E. Pairing

At this stage of the Chase there was one small problem. While it was great to have a group of young enthusiastic volunteers ready to assist in recovering the treasure, we had no idea where it was hidden. With the arrival of the TTOTC we now had all we needed to rectify this situation. A 150-page book and a 24-line poem is all that stood between us and an early retirement.

> *As I have gone alone in there*
> *And with my treasure bold,*
> *I can keep my secret where,*
> *And hint of riches new and old.*
> *Begin it where warm waters halt*
> *And take it in the canyon down*
> *Not far, but too far to walk.*
> *Put in below the home of Brown.*

With supreme belief in our ability to decipher the conundrum we dedicated ourselves to the cause. Making a pact to no longer spend my nights doing work-related activities, we set about solving the Fenn treasure hunt. It took a while to achieve the first inroads into the solution. Fenn had always said the Chase would be solved by someone spending time re-reading the poem and the clues, while examining a map of the search area. To carry out this, I set up a nightly routine. After finishing work and coming home I would have tea with the family before retiring to the war room. I would generally be accompanied by a nice bottle of red wine or sauvignon blanc to keep the mental cogs turning.

It took a number of weeks to attain the initial breakthrough. Like so many others before, I focussed on "Begin it where warm waters halt" as the first clue. Listing all the hot springs located within the Rocky Mountain range I examined each one as a potential contender. There were plenty of likely candidates. This lead to many nights poring over maps of the prospective hot springs and studying the names of the physical features in their general vicinity. The light bulb moment came late one night while examining an area just north of Ouray. There is a well-known hot spring complex at the north end of Ouray township. It is situated beside the Uncompahgre River that flows past the complex and into the canyon running out of town. Many chilly streams flow down out of the San Juan mountains to the east and into the Uncompahgre River.

The Pearl Necklace

Under the magnifying glass I noticed one of the first streams to enter the larger river was named Cutler Creek. Only the previous night I had been trawling through the scrapbooks on Dal Neitzel's site and had noticed there were many seemingly irrelevant stories about spoons, forks, and knifes. The penny dropped and my heart skipped a beat. I grabbed the poem and desperately surveyed it for a reference to cutlery. It took a while but there it was in Line 10 "The end is ever drawing nigh". "Is ever" splits out to become "I sever". This was tenuous so I searched for further evidence to verify this lead. The home of Brown would need to be between the hot springs and Cutler Creek, as well as it being no place for the meek.

It just happens that opposite the road leading up to Cutler Creek is the Ouray Wastewater Treatment Ponds, the ultimate home of brown. It isn't named on most maps but anyone familiar with this sort of facility would recognise the effluent ponds from the air on Google Maps. The use of sewerage ponds as the home of Brown gives an insight into Fenn's roguish sense of humour.

The road up to Cutler Creek is treacherous with massive drop-offs, definitely qualifying it as no place for the meek. There is also however a historical significance that further reiterates its pedigree for this title. In Colorado, in 1879, the Meeker massacre took place, where a band of Uncompahgre Utes attacked the Indian agency on their reservation, killing the Indian agent Nathan Meeker and his 10 male employees and taking five women and children as hostages. The road up to Cutler Creek takes you into the Uncompahgre National Park.

It all fitted perfectly, but unbeknown to me I had fallen into an elaborate trap set by Fenn. It was to cost $40,000 and the next two years of my life. He had deliberately set this as a relatively straight forward solution to his 9-clue puzzle.

The ultimate verification of this solution comes in Line 20 of the poem, "I've done it tired, and now I'm weak." "Done it tired" refers to driving a vehicle to the site, something Fenn repeated constantly. "and now I'm weak" refers to being exhausted, that is, out-of-gas. If you were to leave Fenn's home in Santa Fe in an average sedan full of gas, you would run out of petrol just north of Ouray.

With this nailed-on solution under our belt, we set about organising a trip to retrieve the treasure before any other less deserving person

E. Pairing

might do so. In the remaining time before our departure, research went into finding further evidence to support our solution.

Reading through TTOTC for clues I noticed a glaring anomaly. There was no index listing the chapters within the book. I found this strange when comparing it to other books Fenn had produced. To further interrogate this, I numbered and listed the chapters in TTOTC. There was no bingo moment, but over time I noticed a trend within the chapter titles. Each of them was a cryptic clue in their own right. This was fuel to the fire. Each day I could take away a chapter title and try and decipher it throughout the day. This was magic. When tied up in boring work meetings, I could let my mind wander to the chapter title of the day and be released from the tedium of everyday life.

This process delivered up two repetitive, and critical, features within Fenn's work. The first was the validation of a rule Fenn was to use throughout his writings – leave ME out of it. For any title with ME in it, remove the ME before attempting to solve the clue. Sometimes he would extent this to also include "I". Two years later I would discover the significance and connection between ME and I, but that is a story for later.

The second feature was the repetitive themes within the clues, especially pigs and flies. If I had been a bit more perceptive, I may have realised this could have been a pointer to the well-known saying "Pigs might fly", and the associated implication that this was an elaborate hoax.

By the time we were ready to fly out to America in July 2018, we had managed to extract further vital information from the poem. We had also managed to solve over 50% of the clues from the chapter titles. While the answers to these clues were debatable as to their relevance to the overall solution, what they did do was build a complex picture of mystery and mystique around the chase.

But one clue more than any other had me believing we could not fail in our quest for the treasure. Studying a map of the area upstream of Cutler Creek there were very few prominent features, especially ones with names. One that stood out was Okeson Trailhead. Surely if this was the pathway to the chest it would be hidden within the poem. Analysis of the letters making up the poem show the letters making up OKESON TRAILHEAD are sprinkled within the back end of Line 17 & Line 18.

TO SEek tHe answers I ALREADy KNOw

The left-over letters after spelling out OKESON TRAILHEAD are EK TE ANSWERS YW.

If we reduce the word "answers" to just an A, as in Q&A, we have EK TE A YW.

Re-arranging these we produce YEW TAKE

YEW TAKE OKESON TRAILHEAD

It just happens that Okeson Trailhead takes you high up on to the ridgeline above Cutler Creek giving views out over the San Juan mountains. It also provides access to Winchester Gulch, a narrow gorge descending 1000 metres down into the valley containing Cow Creek on the other side of ridge. Studying Winchester Gulch on Google Earth shows it is the home to colossal rock features, caves, and spectacular waterfalls.

Fenn had said many times, "the treasure is in a place that I want to be my final resting place". Winchester Gulch seemed the perfect location with its secluded beauty facing the morning sun. It was the perfect final burial site.

Going back to the Poem to verify Winchester Gulch as the destination to take to the treasure, we find a number of confirmations. Hidden in Line 3 we find hinT of RICHES NEW, an anagram of WINCHESTER. Then in Line 13 & 14 we find more compelling evidence.

Line 13 finishes with "our quest TO CEASE". To cease can be translated to TWO C's. In response to this clue, Cow Creek fits the brief perfectly. To further cement this as the correct destination Line 14 finishes with the term MARVEL GAZE, an anagram for GRAVEL MAZE, the perfect description for Cow Creek.

With this mountain of evidence, the trip to Colorado couldn't come soon enough. Every time we spend more time examining the poem we would find more references to Ouray. The final verse of the poem is an absolute Ouray benefit. The first line "So hear me all and listen good" is a quote from the movie True Grit, filmed just down the road from Ouray in Ridgway. The second line starts with "Your effort". Fenn often said he hoped for C's at school but always got an "A" for effort. If we trade the effort for "A" here we end up with "Your A", an anagram for Ouray. Line

E. Pairing

3 continues in the same vein, "if YOU ARe", another anagram of Ouray. Finally Line 4 contains a word puzzle that delivers up the same solution. "I give you title to the gold". In the periodic table, gold is AU. To make Ouray, we need the letters ROY. It just happens to turn out that Roy is the French title for King.

So overwhelming was the evidence in support of Ouray as the solution, we were already spending the windfall in our heads.

CHAPTER 4

FENNSPEAK

Over the next few months I dedicated myself to studying everything I could find Forrest Fenn. When you spend many nights with the same person, over time you become like an old married couple, getting to know their innermost thought patterns, how they format their sentences, and how they structure their ideas. In Fenn's case, it was also how he would hide things within his work, and how he would try and lead you down a certain path. It became apparent early on that Fenn had a real passion for the alphabet, words, and the written form. He loved cryptic word puzzles and other literary complexities. It also became apparent Fenn used structure and rules within his own work to give it originality and his own personal stamp. Once these individual idiosyncrasies were learned, recognising, and translating his work became much easier and more pleasurable.

The cryptic rules and structural clues Fenn implanted into his work were numerous, original, and consistent throughout his work, hence the term Fennspeak. The most widespread of these, already mentioned in the previous chapter, is his dictate regarding the use of ME, MY and I. In summary, he directed you should leave ME (and MY and I) out of it. The most widespread use of this directive is in the chapter titles of The Thrill of the Chase. It is where I discovered this trend and then applied it across the rest of his work. To illustrate this, here is a couple of examples:

Chapter 17: My War for Me

For a start, the phase itself is unusual and bit of a give-away. If you remove MY and ME from the title you are left with WAR FOR, a pretty simple anagram of FARROW.

E. Pairing

Many of the answers to the chapter title clues involve pigs, however, in this case the answer is not related to a litter of swine but instead refers to Mia Farrow the well-known actress. Her christian name Mia is an acronym for the military term Missing in Action, and in this context refers to the Unknown Soldier.

Chapter 25: Ode to Peggy Jean

The title of Chapter 25 easily translates to Poem to My Wife

Once the EM (me backwards) and MY are removed from it you are left with PO TO WIFE, an anagram for WIT OF POE. Fenn references the works of Edgar Allan Poe throughout his books and uses aspects of Poe's works within the solution to the chase. We will find out later, having a good understanding of Poe's work is essential to solving the Ouray chase.

These two examples of Fenn's habit of leaving ME out of it are just the tip of the iceberg. He uses the technique over and over again, even on the Cover of The Thrill of the Chase. The book is subtitled A Memoir. Remove the ME and you are left with MOIR. Look up MOIR (surname) on Wikipedia and you will discover the relevance of this clue. If the story of Robert the Bruce and the Knights Templar doesn't get your heart racing, you should go and see a cardiologist.

This leads us to another important habit of Fenn's, the extensive use of Wikipedia. Throughout his books Fenn drops names like autumn leaves. The easiest way to find the relevance of the person or place to the chase is to go to the corresponding Wikipedia page.

Another feature of Fenn's character is his propensity for organisation and structure. This habit is demonstrated strongly in the Poem. Rather than a random assortment of words, the poem is set out in a structured way, with a number of rules governing how it can be deciphered.

The easiest lines in the poem to decipher are those starting with JUST. These lines need no solving, just read them as they are. Next easiest are the lines beginning with SO. These are quotes. Find the source of the quote and it will aid in the interpretation of the chase.

Next pearl of wisdom pertains to the 4 lines with MY in the middle. The letters each side of the MY in these lines are anagrams that are relatively easy to solve, although several throw up multiple possible answers.

Most of the remaining lines are some form of puzzle, anagram, word substitution or association, or literal reference.

Then there are Fenn's stories that fill his publications and scrapbooks. I hate to say it but many of them are fanciful and clearly not true, though Fenn tells them in such a manner, his legions of followers hang onto his every word. As a rule of thumb, the more unbelievable the story, the more likely it is a fabrication to hide a deeper meaning. These hidden clues are incredibly hard to decipher. Unlike his word and letter clues that require a little literary gymnastics, his story clues are complex and often require visualisation and obscure interpretation. Often you are left wondering whether you are off on some strange tangent rather than on the correct path. Due to this, many of the stories remain unsolved, at least to me, their true meaning to be debated over the future years.

Fenn's techniques in hiding clues within his stories are many and varied. It is difficult to provide pointers to solving them due to this diversity. Here is a couple of examples to provide an insight into Fenn's bizarre thought patterns.

In the chapter on page 143 of Once Upon a While Fenn tells a story about a sculptor who sold his works through the Fenn's gallery in New Mexico. Forrest liked his works so much he bought two of the sculptures for his family home. One was two foot tall. The other was 27 inches tall. You don't need to be Einstein to work out one statue was 3 inches taller than the other, but you do need some genius to realise this spells out 3 INCHES T(all)ER. Throughout his works Fenn finds many creative ways to disguise the word WINCHESTER within his stories. It is integral to the solution to the chase and Fenn makes it accessible time and time again, but you are made to work to find it.

By the time Fenn wrote his third treasure book "too far to walk" he was despairing at the lack of progress searchers were making toward the solution. The stories become more transparent, and the clues more bountiful. Most of the solutions from the stories verify the answers to more obscure clues in his earlier books.

Taking Chapter 13 as an example, it is two pages jammed packed with clues. The chapter is named First Home, Mexico Beach House. There is a photo of the house with the inscription "our f rst home". It is clear the I has been removed from the phase, stressing the rule, leave ME or I out of it. This clue goes further into the title. Leaving ME and I out of Mexico we are left with X Co. I took this as an affirmation that the treasure was in Colorado. Next, Fenn tells us he was earning $250 a month minus a $97 car payment. Simple math tells us he was earning

E. Pairing

1836 per year. A quick look through the history books tells us 1836 was the year of the Battle of the Alamo. It was also the year the Colt 45 revolver – the peacemaker - was patented.

In total, across the three books Fenn wrote to promote his treasure hunt, there are 115 chapters, each telling a story with a hidden, usually obscure, meaning. In addition to that the stories are littered with other individual clues. Even though the treasure has been long since found, the relevance of the stories to the final solution will be discussed for many years to come.

After solving many of the clues and puzzles offered up, you build a picture of several dominant themes running throughout the chase. Without giving too much away, Stephen King books and Jeff Bridges movies play a major part in the overall scheme, but one theme dominates more than any other – the Men in Black.

In additional to this, there is Fenn's obvious love of the English alphabet and the letters it contains. Amongst other things, the double Omega symbol alludes to this aspect, being two letters of the Greek alphabet, as is the word 'alphabet' itself, being derived from Alpha and Beta. Throughout his writings Fenn continually makes reference to couplets and triplets of letters. This begins in his very first chapter of TTOTC. He decries his lack of education and how he would like to be a man of letters. In his case this would be a Bachelor of the Arts, a BA. He then goes on to refer to DC Comics and Washington DC. FE features prominently in his works through references to iron, and also his adopted home town of Santa Fe. There is also his love of the artist Fechin, but that is a story for later on. HG is covered off in the cryptic answer to the chapter 'Gold and More'. The solution 'Moreau' is hint at the book 'The Island of Dr. Moreau' by H.G. Wells.

The importance of the letter 'I' is critical to the over solving of the chase, as is the letter 'O'. These letters do not form part of the sequence of couplets and triplets, instead standing on their own.

The significance of JK is discussed later in the book, but rest assured they are important through their association with Agent J and Agent K from Men in Black, and the story regarding a certain first lady.

Through the middle of the alphabet the letter sequences become a little harder to divine. There are numerous references to MiLK, LeMoNs, and New Mexico, but these answers are nowhere as precise or elegant as the earlier examples.

As already mentioned O stands on its own, then QP is accounted for by Fenn's infatuation with Quanah Parker. RST is highly significant through the importance of the word 'rest' in the overall solution. This is probably due to it forming the backend of Fenn's christian name, and his desire to 'Rest in Peace'.

UV light works its way into the back end of the solution, before WXY gives away the biggest clue of them all, the treasure is hidden in Wyoming.

Finally the letter 'Z' also stands alone, providing a pointer especially to a man in black, Zorro, and the mark he left throughout his adventures. It also hints at Zeus, and the significant of Greek mythology to the solution.

And if all that isn't enough to digest, there is one final triple letter that forms part of the all-important final act to the chase, but for now we are four years and many trips away from that point.

CHAPTER 5

SIN CITY

July 2018 finally arrived, and it was time to go collect the treasure.

Our plane touched down in Vegas after a 6-hour flight from Honolulu. It was late, around midnight. Exiting the airport terminal, the air was hot and dry. We caught a cab to Caesars. Out the taxi window we could see a city in full party mode. Neon lights, spectacular fountains, streets heaving with people, unbridled revelry. To add to this, it was Tylers 20th birthday.

We checked in, re-enacting the lobby scene from the Hangover. Once our bags were safely stowed in our room on the 12th floor, we took the lift back down to reception. Joining the partying throng we hit the strip. The plan was simple, we would stay together until about 3am, checking out the nightlife. I would then return to the room and get enough sleep to be ready to drive us to Colorado the next day via the Grand Canyon and Monument Valley. The rest of the team could stay out and party until the wee hours, catch a few hours shut eye then sleep in the car on the way to the Canyon. What could possibly go wrong?

Leaving Caesars, we stood on the raised terrace looking out across to the Bellagio with its majestic fountains. The view and the warm night air were intoxicating. After a session of selfies, group shots, and social media posts, we descended down onto the Strip. We had no plan as to where we were going and let the crowd drag us here and there through a procession of bars. The crazy individuals, endless mirrors, flashing slot machines, topless dancers, cheap drinks, vibrant music, and desert heat created an out-of-this world experience.

The Pearl Necklace

After a couple of hours of this excitement, we were having the time-of-our-lives. Spilling out of an overcrowded bar, we found ourselves standing in front of a massive pink neon sign. It was a giant lotus flower with the word 'Flamingo' emblazoned above and below it.

"Flamingo's," I exclaimed, arms spread wide as if at some sacred site.

"Genius," Colt replied, with no attempt to hide his sarcasm.

"It's a sign," I continued.

"Utter genius," Colt continued, with even deeper sarcasm.

I could pick up the vibe that the younger generation were not in the mood for another lecture on the relevance of this moment to the grander Forrest Fenn universe. Not wanting to be the killjoy to what had so far been an awesome night, I suggested they carry on to the next bar while I undertook this pilgrimage, before returning to Caesars to sleep as planned. Reluctantly they agree and I watched as they disappeared into the Beach Bar.

Suddenly alone, I ventured into the Flamingo establishment. In the chapter of TFTW named "Sunday kind of love" Fenn had told one of his wild stories regarding a late-night rendezvous with a beautiful woman at Flamingo's. Her name was Fran Warren, a famous singer at the time. The relevance of the story was lost on me. I was hoping now there might be something of importance within Flamingo's that would cast some light on this mystery.

I made my way to Bugsy's Bar, named for Benjamin "Bugsy" Seigel, a big-time mob gangster who in the 1940's had fought to get the Flamingo Hotel completed, setting the scene for Las Vegas to eventually become the gambling capital of the world. The bar was relatively quiet compared to the streets and other bars down the Strip. Ordering a beer from the barman I scanned the room, racking my brain as to why Fenn would use this setting for one of his fanciful tales. Was there possibly a connection between Bugsy Seigel and the answer to one of Fenn's TTOTC title puzzles?

"Totem Café Caper" had been one of the easier TTOTC chapter titles to decipher. Following the golden rule of removing ME or I, we are left with Tot Café Caper. A tot is a baby, café is an anagram for face. "Baby Face" Nelson was a well-known gangster in the 1930's who killed more FBI agents than any other gangster. Was there a possible connection between "Baby Face Nelson" and Bugsy Seigel? All this was intriguing but really didn't take me anywhere. Downing my drink, I headed for the exit.

E. Pairing

Time was moving on, and I needed sleep before our trip east later today. Leaving the bar, I looked at the directions pole for the route back to Caesars. It was there I noticed a sign, directly below the one pointing the way to the Flamingo wedding chapel. It read "Bugsy Seigel Memorial". What the hell I thought, I'm only here once. Walking briskly down the path indicated, I passed the Chapel which was still in full swing despite it being 3:22 in the morning. A dimly lit walkway disappeared around the side of the chapel. A couple were making out vigorously up against the wall of the chapel. It looked like a re-enactment of the scene from the Godfather. 'Only in Vegas' I thought as I put my head down and scurried past. The path led to a quiet garden behind the chapel. There, within a knee-high circular wall, was a stone cairn with a bronze plaque embedded in it. Under the headline "The Bugsy Building" the inscription read:

"On this site, Benjamin "Bugsy" Siegel's original Flamingo Hotel stood from December 26, 1946, until December 14th, 1993. The hotel, which housed 77 rooms, including the notorious Mr. Siegel's "Bugsy Suite" or "Presidential Suite" as it was sometimes referred to, was unique in more ways than one. The windowpanes, for instance, were bullet proof, and, although there was only one entrance to the top-floor suite, there were five possible exits. This included a hidden ladder leading from the hallway closet to a basement tunnel, which led to an underground garage, where Bugsy allegedly had a chauffeured getaway car awaiting at all times. But Mr. Siegel's preoccupation with safety and escape routes proved to be geographically misplaced. On June 20, 1947, 300 miles from Las Vegas, at the Beverley Hills mansion of his girlfriend, Virginia Hill, Bugsy was killed in a hail of gunfire by unknown assailants. Since that day, the Flamingo has changed ownership 4 times, including its final sale from Park Place Entertainment in 2005."

I sat on the low wall and weighed up the significance of what I had just read. Nothing came to me as the passionate moaning and groaning from the darkened pathway made it hard to concentrate. After 10 minutes the noise subsided, and the coast was clear. I stood up and made my way back to Caesars. It was later than planned, about 4am. By now the mood of the Strip had changed. The sidewalks were strewn with litter, and there were numerous bodies passed out in the gardens along the way. Striding purposefully and avoiding any eye contact, I made my way hastily to the hotel and up to our room on the 12th floor. Absolutely spent and without undressing, I collapsed onto one of the two double beds in the room.

Sometime later I was awoken by the room door being unlocked. Squinting at the red numbers on the bedside clock I could barely discern the time. Eventually my eyes came into focus, and I could see it was 5:35. Making a futile effort to be quiet, Tyler and Briar-Rose banged their way across the room to the bed closer to the windows. Eventually they managed to get under the covers, and silence returned to the world.

After what seemed like 5 minutes "Take Me to Church" by Hozier blared from my cell phone, tucked away under my pillow. The pre-set alarm had been set for 9:30. Despite the copious beers consumed on the Strip the night before, it was immediately apparent I was the only one on the bed. I was wide awake instantly, hoping to see Colt passed out on one of the chairs in the room. No such luck. Knowing most of the bars were long shut by now, I had visions of him passed out in a garden alongside the other victims I had seen on my way home. Visions from the movie The Hangover were playing out in my head.

"Colt, where are you?" I messaged hurriedly on my phone. No reply

"Colt, are you okay?" I messaged again. No reply.

Feeling the tension within me rising, I tried ringing. His cell phone went straight to answer.

Getting up off the bed I was thankful for not having undressed before crashing out.

"Rosie, wake up."

"What time is it?" she murmured without opening her eyes.

"Colt hasn't come home."

"Shit," she replied, "we left him at the Beach Bar. He was chatting up some girl."

"Christ, some things never change. He could be anywhere. Do you know if she was a local or a tourist?"

"She was with a group of girls on a Hen's Party weekend from Idaho. They were staying here as well."

I pulled the cord to open the curtains and stared blankly down at the pool area below. Despite it being only 9:45 the expansive landscape was already bustling with pool goers taking in the 30-degree sunshine. Reaching into my hiking pack I extracted my trusty binoculars.

Feeling a little uneasy about viewing the scantily attired individuals in and around the pools from afar, I methodically worked from one end

E. Pairing

of the area to the other. There were a couple of instances where it was difficult not to dwell longer than was acceptable, but finding Colt was the priority.

Just when I was looking to jack it in, a young man with blondish hair came into focus. Adjusting the glasses, the image became sharper. Sure enough, it was Colt, still in his nightclub attire, stretched out on a poolside lounger. On the lounger beside him was a barely clad young girl. They were holding hands while gazing into each other eyes.

"Jackpot," I declared, thrusting the binoculars to Tyler. "Don't lose sight of him. He's on the third lounger from the end," pointing through the window at the line of chairs on the far side of the main pool. With that, I made for the door and the elevator down to the ground floor.

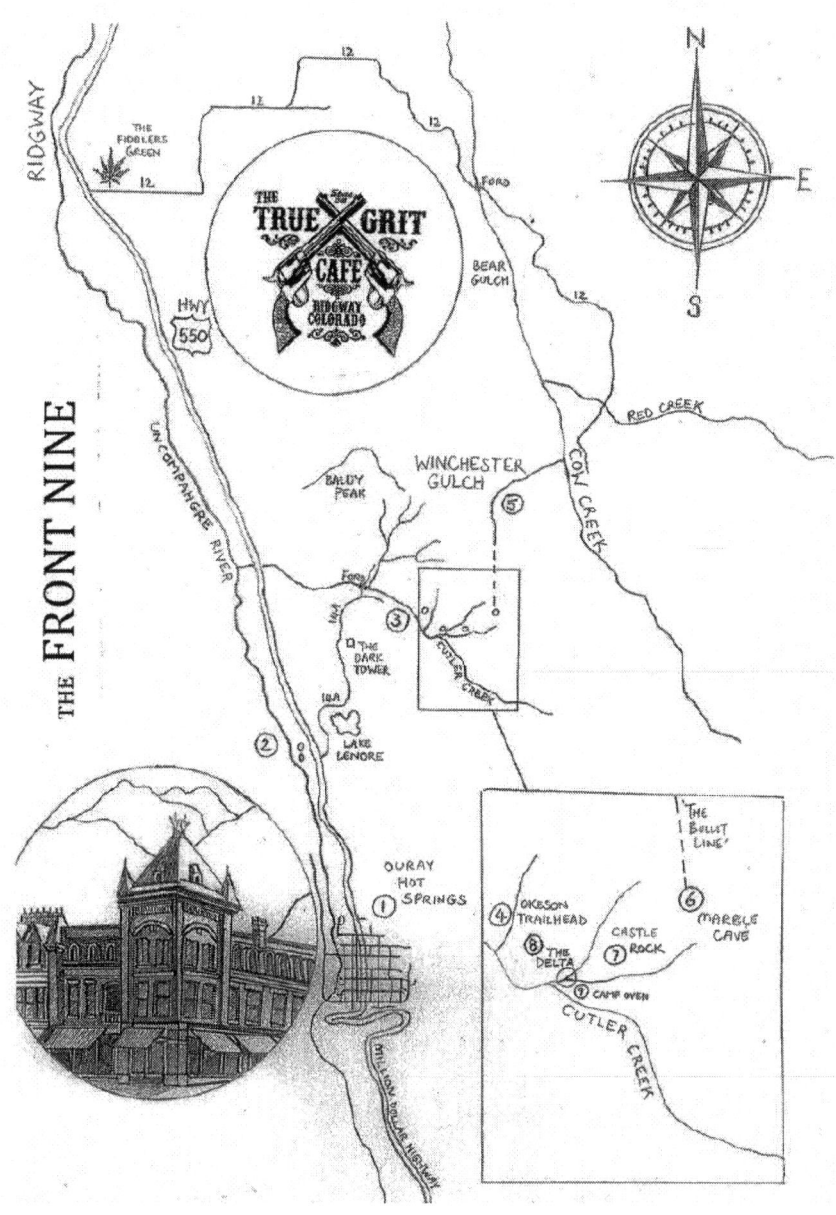

CHAPTER 6

FIDDLERS GREEN

Since leaving Australia I had one nagging fear. It was the thought of driving 1500 miles on the wrong side of the road. However, the hardest thing about the drive to Ouray turned out to be finding the rental car outlet in Vegas. We trudged down the strip for an hour in the searing heat, dragging our suitcases, looking like the archetypal tourists, in search of the Budget Car Rental stand. After numerous enquiries we were directed back into Caesars Palace, the stand being less than two hundred metres from where we had originally started 2 hours previous.

Out of respect to Fenn's home town, and as a positive omen to finding the treasure, we hired a Santa Fe. Had the girl behind the desk known of our intentions it is doubtful she would have handed over the keys. On the policy it stated clearly the vehicle was not to be driven off-road, but it was hardly likely we would recover the treasure if we stuck to that directive. We piled our bags and packs into the shiny, near-new vehicle and drove out into the 40-degree Nevadan heat. As driver, I had one critical rule imprinted on my mind, and printed in inch-high letters on a memo note on the steering wheel – tight right, long left. Coming from Australia, and now driving on the opposite side of the road, this instruction was vital for our survival.

The drive to Ouray was spectacular and not without incident. We had deliberately chosen to go via the Grand Canyon and Monument Valley. This was not only to take in the incredible scenery but to avoid having to take one of the most dangerous roads in America, the Million Dollar highway, supposed named due to it costing that amount per mile to create. An alternate suggestion was, it was named that for having to pay someone that amount of money to drive it. It would have been the quickest route into Ouray when coming from the south, but we had chosen to skirt around the mountains and take the safer route, entering it from the north. Ouray is a spectacular town sitting north-south within a small box canyon. It is quite unusual in that the south end of the town is much higher than the north end. The million-dollar highway comes in from the south over a high mountain road, winding down the side of the mountain and into the top end of the main street. The main street is long, wide, and runs straight downhill to where the road from the north enters. Old brick shops, bars, and other heritage buildings line the street from top to bottom. It is the ultimate wild west town, and we had booked into St. Elmos, the most quintessential wild west hotel in all of Colorado.

Built in 1898 St. Elmo's is situated high up at the south end of town. Entering Ouray from the north we drove up the steady incline of the bustling main street, managing to find a park right outside. Unpacking our bags and packs from the Santa Fe, we shuffled through the front door of the hotel. Driving through Ouray with its historic brick buildings and stunning granite cliffs had got the blood pumping, but the interior of St. Elmo's took it to another level. The entry area was a dark lounge with ornate Victorian décor complete with purple velvet wallpaper, and a cut-crystal chandelier. The check in with its black marble counter was dominated by the huge skull of a longhorn steer hanging above it. To top it off, a denim clad seductress with tasselled waist coat, longhorn belt buckle, and large black cowboy hat leaned invitingly on one end of the counter, chatting to the clerk. He was also dresses like he had just stepped out of a Clint Eastwood movie.

"Mr. Pairing," I announced, offering my hand to the clerk, "here for the next 4 days."

"Aussies," purred Denim Belle, "I love a man from down under."

"I bet you do," I replied, struggling to find an appropriate response.

"Are you here for long," Denim Belle asked with a smile.

"A few days hiking in the mountains," I replied with my best poker face.

"Sure you are. That's what they all say. Don't worry, your secret will be safe with me darling."

"Room 1," said the clerk gruffly, nodding toward the door we had passed on our way in. The rugged hand that had crushed my fingers

E. Pairing

minutes earlier pushed two keys across the marble counter. He then turned and disappeared into the back office.

"Looking for somewhere to eat out tonight?" Denim Belle enquired, "The Italian next door is very good."

"Sure," I offered back. "We've been on the road all day. I could eat a horse."

"I bet you could," she purred back, "Enjoy your stay." With that, she turned on her heels and disappeared through the door behind her.

I hardly slept a wink that night. The chicken parmigiani wasn't a great choice, and the muggy box canyon air, and thoughts of Fenn's treasure had me tossing and turning all night, until giving up completely. As the sun came up I got out of bed and repacked my hiking bag with the essentials for the day ahead. Bear spray, knife, rope, whistle, compass, map, bags for the treasure.

It was several hours before the kids finally emerged. They were in no hurry to go anywhere. We sat around the dining table and had breakfast with the supplies we had bought from Walmart the previous day. The conversation was sparse and stilted. The late night and long drive from Vegas had taken its toll. Outside the door, we could hear the hotel quests coming and going through the reception area.

Eventually we had our bags packed and were ready to venture out. The anticipation started to build once we were in the Santa Fe and driving down the main street. Past the hot springs where warm waters halt we headed down the canyon stopping at the Waste water ponds, the home of Brown. Directly opposite was the road up into the Uncompahgre National Park. In real life, it was much steeper and narrower than it appeared on Google Maps. I said a prayer that we wouldn't meet any traffic coming the other way and gunned it up the track. After a short time, we came to a quaint lake set in the side of the hill. Around the lake were several chalets. Off to the left a side track, country road 14A, crossed a small bridge and turned to gravel. There was a layby for a horse trekking outfit offering rides up into the San Juan mountains. Then the track became much steeper and even narrower. The drop off the side of the trail was becoming greater and more perilous with every second. After 100 yards I stopped the vehicle and applied the handbrake. Looking around I was met by 3 faces shocked white in abject terror.

"I don't think this is a great idea," stammered Colt. "What if we meet someone coming down?"

We all let that thought sink in for a minute, then I stuck the car in reverse and backed slowly down the track to the layby. "It's a long walk from here but at least we won't die", I said in an effort to lift the morale. A little colour had returned to their faces as we donned our packs and set off up the track on foot.

The views up and down the canyon valley became more spectacular as we tramped up the road. Being able to see the sheer drop off the side first hand reinforced our decision to park up and walk the route. After 500 yards we reached the high point of the trail before it turned sharply to the right and headed between two hills up into the mountains. Incredibly we were presented with two amazing sights at this point. Someone had parked a diminutive silver caravan on the outside of the bend. There was no towing-vehicle to be seen, with only chocks under the wheels stopping the caravan from disappearing into the abyss. I imagined sitting within the caravan, alone, in a massive thunderstorm at night. "Does everyone in this place have a death wish?" I thought to myself.

On the other side of the road, and a little further down the slope, we had passed a wooden tower built on the hillside high above the track. It seemed out-of-place in the landscape, as if built there to serve some special but unknown purpose. It was 15 feet square at the base and tapered inwards as it rose to its apex, 30 feet from the ground. Rough boards had been hammered onto the posts making entry into the structure near impossible.

Pondering these two mysteries we continued our hike up to Cutler Creek. By now the path had levelled out and the walking was much easier. The track entered a forested area and through the trees to the left the creek could be seen running down to the canyon to join the Uncompahgre River.

By the time we reached the campground we had been walking for about ¾ an hour. We were greeted with a large sign warning of black bears in the area. Beside it was a circle of rocks surrounding a darkened mound of ash. The large meadow cum campground was deserted. Consulting the map, it became clear we had at least another 2 hours tramping over mountainous terrain to reach our intended destination, Winchester Gulch.

E. Pairing

"Didn't Fenn say he parked his car and walked twice to the treasure site in an afternoon," offered Tyler. "I'm not sure an 80-year-old man could manage this."

"Maybe he hired a horse," suggested Briar-Rose.

"Good thought, but if you look at the map, he could have driven up Cow Creek to the bottom of Winchester Gulch. He would only have to walk 500 yards from there to the treasure site," I replied.

"Why are we going this way then," retorted Tyler.

"Because the poem says to take Okeson Trailhead," I said defensively.

"Make up your mind, is it Okeson trail, or Cow Creek?, I suggest we vote on it."

"Okay, whose for Cow Creek?" I announced, trying to be decisive.

Tyler and Briar-Rose half—heartedly raised their hands.

"Cow Creek it is then," I proclaimed, not wanting to go to a deadlocked vote.

With that we headed back to the car. The walk gave me time to go over the revised plan in my head.

We'd need to drive north to Ridgway, then take Country Road 12 to its end. From there a dirt track would take us to a ford crossing Cow Creek. Hopefully the water level would allow us to drive through the ford. The track then roughly followed the creek south for about 3 miles until it came out at a gravel maze below the Gulch. We would park up there, wade the creek, and head up the Gulch.

The drive to Ridgway was uneventful, retracing the route we'd taken the night before on the way into Ouray.

Country Rd 15 was also accommodating but that all changed when we got onto the dirt track past its end. Recent rain had turned the dirt to mud and large potholes made driving treacherous. Questions were starting to be raised as to the wisdom of this plan, and what the rental company would say if they could see us now. Just when we thought things couldn't get worse we arrived at the ford.

"No fucken way," came the first comment that began a torrent of expletives from the passenger seats.

The water was about a foot deep across a bed of large river stones. Overall the "creek" was about 60 feet wide, split into two sections with a car width island in the middle.

We stopped on the edge of the water and weighed up the pros and cons of moving forward. The overwhelming sentiment was we shouldn't venture into the creek.

Turning my cap backwards I thought, "We've come this far, I whispered to myself, "No guts, no glory," masking my inner fear that this could be a really big mistake. I revved the engine and charged into the stream. Almost immediately the car lost traction and drifted sideways downstream. My heart was now beating out of my chest. Taking my foot momentarily off the accelerator, I then applied it more gently. Somehow the car found traction and moved forward, lurching over the rocks under the water. It rose up and bounced onto the island midstream. Before we could have second thoughts I continued forward back into the water. Luckily the second half of the stream was shallower, and we safely negotiated it without incident, reaching the far bank with much hollering and high fives.

This exuberance was short-lived as the full landscape into which we had just entered came into view.

Cow Creek ran down the bottom of a mountain valley, precipitous bluffs forming walls on either side. The track didn't follow the creek at water level as expected but could be seen in the distance about half way up the 1000-foot cliffs.

"No fucken way," came the now familiar refrain from the back seat.

"No guts, no glory," I echoed back, steering the Santa Fe up the mountain trail.

It didn't take long to realise this was a grave mistake.

The ruts grew deeper and muddier the further we went. The trail up to Cutler Creek had been child's play compared to this route. We were barely a quarter the way up the track when the overwhelming consensus was to turn around, the only problem being the track was barely wide enough for a car. We pressed on at a snail's pace praying we wouldn't disappear over the edge and into the trees clinging to the side of the mountain. Eventually we came to a tight bend with a short run-off into the hillside. We were able to drive past then reverse into it, revving to get the rear end of the car up the bank. We then inched forward, executing the turn to head back down the path. The collective relief in the car was palpable. We slowly made our way back to creek level where we parked up to weigh our options.

E. Pairing

Studying the map of the area we estimated it was 2 miles up the creek bed to the base of Winchester Gulch. Collectively we agreed this was the best alternative. We found a spot where we could stow the car within the trees and undergrowth, unpacked our gear, and headed down to the water.

The plan to walk up the streambed proved to be a lot harder in practice than anticipated. Branches overhanging from the banks on either side of the creek made walking up the stream the only option. Progress was slower than planned, but this soon became the least of our worries. The groaning and snuffling in the creek side bushes confirmed the place name on the map, Bear Gulch, was still relevant.

Staying as far away as possible from the banks we stuck to the centre of the stream. The further from the car we went, the greater the sense of unease. After an eternity we came upon a low gravel island in the middle of the waterway. A large pile of bear skat on the sandy shore turned our sense of unease to apoplectic shock. It was the size of a dinner plate, filled with undigested red berries. To top it off the bear pat was still steaming. The grumbling from the bushes intensified to a crescendo. We contracted into a tight huddle as if preparing for imminent attack. Suddenly 10 yards upstream, a huge black bear came crashing out of the bushes and into the stream. Turning to face us the bear reared up on its back legs.

"Don't move," I stammered, "Make yourself big," I continued, remembering the instructions from the local hiking booklet. One reason we had come as a group of four was it is extremely rare for bears to attack groups of four or larger, though I wasn't sure this bear was aware of that fact.

The bear charged forward and clawed the ground only yards in front of us.

I fumbled for the knife hanging off my belt. I could see Colt out of the corner of my eye reaching for the spray can on the side of his pack.

Pawing the ground more furiously the bear edged closer.

Unexpectedly, two young cubs appeared out of the bushes on the opposite bank. Instantly, the large bear wheeled away and bounded across the island and into the water by the cubs. After some routine sniffing and snorting the reunited threesome disappeared back into the shrubbery.

The Pearl Necklace

Their departure did little to remove the overwhelming fear. We were frozen to the spot like four stone statues, our hearts pounding out of our chests. Briar-Rose was gasping hard for air, struggling to breathe while Tyler comforted her.

Keen to depart the bear zone, I somehow convinced the others to continue upstream, though the decision was definitely not unanimous. Travelling in that direction was short-lived, lasting only until the next sand and gravel island. There in the wet sand were the unmistakeable prints of a mountain lion. It was an impossible task to convince the group to go any further.

Heading back to the car, for some mad reason, we decided it was wisest to walk in the water to avoid the mountain lions, bears, and any other local predators that may be present. This made for slow, but presumably safe, progress.

Ironically the creek offered up one final treat. Large worms could be seen in the water swimming around our bare lower legs. Without thinking I reached down and scooped one up in my hand. Only then did I see the proportionately large fangs protruding from the "worms" mouth. Only once it had sunk its teeth into my finger did I realise the worms were in fact baby water snakes.

Once safely back in the car still parked in the undergrowth there were tears of unrestrained relieve. The fact we still had to negotiate the ford across the river was irrelevant. So what if we wrote-off a new rental car, at least we would still be alive.

We need not have worried. The ford crossing was uneventful and before long we were heading into Ridgway. The Santa Fe was unrecognisable, completely covered in mud, but we were ready to celebrate our bear attack survival. On the way in we had noticed a cannabis dispensary The Fiddlers Green on the outskirts of town. This was a unique opportunity for us Australians, so we swung into the carpark and fronted up to the veranda. Heading inside it took a moment for our eyes to adjust to the dark interior and the smoke-laden ambience. A long wooden counter created a barrier to a wall covered with glass jars filled with the sacred weed. Snoop Doggs twin brother stood behind the counter, arms splayed wide, his ring encrusted hands palms down on the glass topped bench.

"Welcome my friends, to the show that never ends, come inside, come inside."

E. Pairing

He guided us through a bead curtain into the inner sanctum. It was even smokier and more atmospheric than the outer shopfront. Through the haze you could make out several groups sampling the establishments wares. Snoop 2 handed us each a menu and motioned toward a half-circle booth in the back corner of the room. Following his direction, we made our way across the room already feeling the heady effect of the sweet fumes. Collapsing into the domed leather seats our sense of safety and security was now complete. The next hour was spent sampling various species from the top shelf, before purchasing a range of cannabis products and edibles. Comfortably numb we mooched out into the late afternoon air, jumped into the Santa Fe, and headed back up the canyon to Ouray.

CHAPTER 7

HUNTING THE SNIPE

A day like this now demanded a night to match. A night not celebrating the finding of treasure but a night celebrating surviving a near death experience. It was much publicised that 5 people had already perished attempting to find Fenn's treasure. We were glad not to have become a gruesome addition to the tally.

On arrival back in town we headed straight to the roof-top bar of one of the local establishments. It was busy so we had to queue at the crowded bar for drinks. Two barmen worked tirelessly to keep up with the demand. Both were distinctive in their own way. The taller of the two was black which was fairly unusual in these parts, while the other stood out for the patch he was wearing over his left eye. He also wore a "Mountains are Calling" T-shirt.

The beer they served us was divine, and the hamburgers we ordered were also heaven sent. Sitting there in the late afternoon sun, looking out over that box canyon town was one of those special moments when you are at peace with the world. We still had two days left to find a way into Winchester Gulch and life was good.

A couple of rounds later and the sun had disappeared behind late afternoon clouds. A storm rolled in from the south and rain began to fall. We relocated to the bar downstairs to avoid getting wet and ordered more drinks. Eyepatch was still serving, and my mind started working overtime. Any true student of the Chase would have watched the original True Grit movie. It starred John Wayne and was filmed in and around Ridgway. In the movie John Wayne played Reuben (Colt) Cogburn, a

E. Pairing

US Marshal who worn a patch over his left eye. It seemed hell of a coincidence that here was a barman, wearing an eyepatch and sporting a T-shirt with a quote from the Fenn poem on it. The temptation got too much for me and I struck up a conversation with an old-timer sitting in a corner of the bar. After exchanging pleasantries, I enquired about the patched bartender. The wizened local narrowed his eyes and looked at me suspiciously. "I've got no clue what you are talkin' about," he drawled, "Johnny lost that eye in a bow accident years ago. As for his T-shirt, they sell them across the road at the Cut Price Mart."

It quickly became apparent there was an unwritten rule in these parts not to talk about Fenn's treasure. You could hint at it but making direct reference to it seemed to be a sin punishable by exclusion from any conversation. Supposedly there were 35,000 people looking for the treasure, but none of the locals would admit to knowing anything about it.

It all reminded me of my first visit to America 20 years prior.

I had travelled to rural Iowa to help commission a new factory. The people were warm and friendly, and grateful for me trekking half way across the globe to assist in bringing employment to their struggling region. The first weekend arrived, and they invited me to go snipe hunting with them. I immediately recognised this as a ruse going by various names all around the world. Not wanting to rain on their fun I went along with the plan. We drove out to a bush area several miles out of town. Circling around to the far side of the copse of trees, they gave me a sack and positioned me at the end of a channel coming out of the bush to catch the elusive snipe. The rest of the group disappeared into the bush to flush out the prey. I knew all too well they were going to find their way back through the bush to the pick-up trucks and head back into town. I figured I could leave as soon as they were out of sight and take a direct route across country back into town. I was then faced with a dilemma. Should I go back to my motel and hole up there, leaving them to worry about where I had got to, or play along and go to the pub to be derided for falling for their rural prank?

As they disappeared out of range I bolted and jumped the fence into the neighbouring farm, taking care to stay out of view. Running head down along a shallow creek bed I could see the trail of dust from the pick-ups as they sped toward Allerton. Just as I felt safe to run upright without fear of being seen, a voice boomed out behind me "Where do you think you are going?" My heart leapt into my mouth, and I spun around to see an old cocky leaning against a fence with a shotgun under his arm. "Lost your way have you Sonny."

"Just taking a shortcut back to town," I stammered, my heart still beating out of my chest.

"What's the sack for?" the OC enquired.

"Snipe hunting," I replied.

This bought a huge grin to OC's face. "That old turnip, surely you didn't fall for that did ya," OC asked with a laugh.

"Of course not," I replied "Just playing along for the hell of it."

"Good," came back OC, "You don't look the kinda guy who fall for that malarkey. How about we play a little joke of our own?"

"What do you have in mind?" I enquired, warming to my new friend.

"There's a large prairie kingsnake living down by my hen house. How about we put it in ya sack and take it back to town."

I almost wet myself at the suggestion, not due to the humor of the idea but the sheer dread of handling reptiles. I had only ever seen a couple of snakes back in Australia and both times I had almost died of fright.

"Don't worry cobber," drawled the OC, picking up on the Aussie accent, "this critters pretty harmless."

Within the next twenty minutes OC had managed to capture the snake, put it in the sack, and drive me the 3 miles to the Legion bar in Allerton. He dropped me out front and went to find a park out back. "Hang around 5 minutes before going in," he advised, "I want to be inside to see this go down."

I reached into the tray of the pick-up and carefully grabbed the sack. It was reasonably heavy at arm's length, and the movement of the contents confirmed its existence.

Walking into the bar one of the factory group spotted me immediately and greeted me loudly, causing most of the 40-strong crowd to turn and stare.

"What you got in the sack," he cried, "managed to catch yourself a snipe." Raucous laughter filled the bar. "I think so," I stuttered, beginning to question the sanity of the plan. Before I could have second thoughts I inverted the sack and dropped the contents onto the floor.

Pandemonium broke loose. People jumped onto the barstools, leaners, and the pool table, while others ran for the doors. Equally afraid,

E. Pairing

the snake slithered across to the nearest wall, then followed the wall until it found an opening, the doorway out into the back carpark.

I couldn't understand why, but the reception we received in Ouray when raising the topic of the Chase brought this incident back to mind. Anyway, my fruitless attempt to extract information from the old-timer in the bar had dampened the mood a tad. We agreed it was time to cash in our chips and head back to our lodgings. It was still raining outside and now dark as well. Making sure the main street was clear, we ducked our heads and ran across the road and up the footpath to St Elmos. Once inside, the kids crashed out on their beds. I decided to retreat to the spa pool out the back of the hotel. It was nothing flash but the view from the pool was amazing. The western wall of the box canyon towered above the spa less than a quarter mile away.

After donning my board shorts I headed out back to the fenced off spa. Unlatching the head high wooden gate, I entered the confined area. There in the pool was Denim Belle, reclining against the side of the spa with her arms spread out wide, and her deep red bikini leaving little to the imagination.

"Dundeee," DB beamed, "Welcome to my water hole." Unable to retreat, I slipped into the water and took up a position directly opposite her, with my back to the moonlit rock bluffs.

She drew in her arms and slid across the pool like an alligator approaching its prey. Suddenly she was clinging to my side, her free hand working overtime below the water. I had visions of her putting me in a deathroll and taking me to the bottom.

"You know the treasures Up Black Bear Pass," she whispered, before devouring my earlobe with her voluptuous lips.

I looked quickly down, her ample cleavage only inches from my face. Her hand gripped the inside of my thigh, and my ability to resist was being seriously tested.

Suddenly an eruption of colour burst through the gate. It was Colt, clearly stoned out of his tree. He was clutching a large milkshake in his left hand, and spilling cheezies from a bag in his other.

"Dad, you old seadog," he blurted out, "Is there room for another one in there?"

As if by magic, Denim Belle had found her way back to the other side of the pool without me noticing.

"Sure, the more the merrier," she replied with a hint of sarcasm.

Colt stripped off his T-shirt and stumbled his way into the pool, somehow managing this manoeuvre without spilling a drop of his shake.

"Nice landing," DB congratulated Colt. "Oh, I love your nipple piercings," she continued.

Realising my growing irrelevance to the situation and preferring not having to watch my only son get devoured by a dangerous predator I decided to retreat to the sanctuary of our room.

"Remember we are heading out early tomorrow Colt," I advised as I extricated myself from the swamp, "we're leaving around 9 o'clock."

"'No worries," Colt fired back, unaware he was about to be eaten alive.

Back in the room the enormity of the day took its toll and I collapsed onto the double bed. BR and Tyler had obviously shared in the Fiddlers Green delights with Colt as muffled laughter emanated from the adjoining room. A plan still had to be made for tomorrow but that could wait until then. I turned out the light and descended into a deep sleep.

The next day arrived too soon. Colt stumbled in just as the rest of us were rising. He looked like he had just survived 10 rounds with Mike Tyson. Disappearing into the bathroom, he showered and tidied himself up.

Over breakfast we devised a plan for the day. Rather than repeat the errors of the previous day, we decide to approach one of the off-road hire companies in Ouray and see if they could transport us up to the Cutler Creek campground.

Thankfully they were receptive to the idea and for $100 agreed to deliver us to the top of route 14A. They were even happy to come and pick us up 5 hours later for no further charge.

Dropping us beside the ford across Cutler Creek, at the entry to the camp ground, we made our first bad decision of the day. Our map of the area showed the shortest route to Winchester Gulch was to cross the ford and take Storm Gulch Trailhead up to Short Cut Trail. It would lead us up onto the ridge from where we could descend down into Winchester. I had figured taking Short Cut may have been a physical representation of the saying "Cut to the Chase".

The trek up Storm Gulch Trail proved to be demanding. The exertions of the previous day, the stifling heat, and the thin air at 10,000 feet soon took its toll. After half an hour I was huffing and puffing like an old mountain goat. We had cans of oxygen to deal with this

E. Pairing

eventuality, but they did little to help the situation. The rest of the team were clearly worried about my ability to conquer the demands of reaching Baldy Ridge and descending into Winchester Gulch. On top of this, the presence of bears in the area was obvious and every sound from the surrounding bush was treated with suspicion.

After about an hour, we were two thirds the way up to the ridge, however the track was getting narrower and steeper, and the drops off the side more precipitous. Incredibly there were horseshoe prints in the mud showing the trekking company used the route as access to the tops. My stamina was being sorely tested and I would have given my kingdom for a mount.

Stopping for a cup of tea, we were perturbed to see black clouds rolling in from the south. It was clear a thunderstorm was brewing and being high in the Rockies is not the place to be when lightning is about. As the storm was still distant we agreed to push on up to the ridge and reconsider once we had reached that milestone.

Another half hour of hard slog and we ascended onto the ridge. The view was magnificent looking out over the snow-capped San Juan Mountains to the east. It was clear why Fenn would have chosen the valley below as his last resting place. It was secluded and serene, yet spectacularly beautiful.

We however were faced with a small problem. Not only was the sky becoming increasingly darker, but time was against us. It had taken us one and a half hours to ascend the ridge, and I for one was extremely fatigued. We quickly did the math. Another hour to descend down into Winchester Gulch. An hour to locate the treasure. An hour and a half to climb back out of the Gulch, then an hour to descend back down to the campground. We were going to be an hour late for our ride back to Ouray. Rain was starting to fall, and the thunder claps were getting louder. There was also the ever-present doubt of how an octogenarian could have travelled this route twice in an afternoon carrying a chest full of gold and treasure.

Weighing up all the variables we came to the conclusion the only way Fenn could have carried out the mission was on horse-back. From his books we knew he was an experienced horseman, but unfortunately we didn't have any mounts at our disposal at this point in time.

Regrettably, the tough decision was made for us to return to base.

The Pearl Necklace

Retracing our steps down the Storm Gulch track there was the realisation we would be returning home without the treasure. This was a bitter pill to swallow as many family and friends were monitoring our progress eagerly from afar. There was no disguising the disappointment and the was mood matched the gloomy atmosphere surrounding us. I had to make the frank admission we had gone off half-cocked, and it was quite prophetic how accurate this statement would prove to be.

CHAPTER 8

THE LONG RIDE HOME

The concept of the long ride home featured prominently in Fenn's first book The Thrill of the Chase. It had grown out of his childhood holidays where his family would travel from Temple Texas to Yellowstone for the summer break then return the 1400 miles home at the end of their adventures.

This fitted beautifully into the chase where thousands of prospective treasure hunters would return home empty-handed at the end of their endeavours. For us this was even more pronounced than most. We had a 600-mile drive back to Las Vegas, then a 16-and-a-half-hour flight back to Australia via Hawaii.

On the back of the expectation we would be $2M richer, the drive back to Las Vegas was somewhat subdued. We overnighted in Green River. This actually raised our spirits as what was once a thriving tourist stop-off was now a rundown backwater, but for us this was the real America.

We stumbled into the local watering hole. It was one of those places where the jukebox stops the minute a stranger walks through the door. Once the locals realised we weren't there to steal their children, we were able to order a drink and have a massive feed of mainly prime American beef.

The drive in the morning to Vegas was cathartic. Working through the five stages of grief we had moved rapidly to acceptance. Acceptance we hadn't found the treasure, hadn't even reached our target destination.

The Pearl Necklace

This was tempered with the knowledge the treasure was still out there, still available to be found in the future.

We cranked up Garth on the car stereo and blasted down the highway through Utah, stopping in Beaver for lunch and to buy a "I love Beaver" T-shirt, before heading back into Sin City.

Vegas was still sweltering under 45-degree heat as we drove in from the north. It was 7 o'clock in the evening and the strip was just coming to life. We dropped the rental back at Budget and checked into Caesars. Tonight's plan was simple. We were going to stay out and wash away our disappointment. At 6am, we would recover our bags from the room and taxi to the airport.

Once on the plane the emotions became quite raw. We were heading home without the treasure. Deep down, I was relieved we had survived the adventure and we were all on the plane in one piece, safely headed back home. Obviously there was a huge underlying disappointment the treasure hadn't been found. The kids had relied on my confidence in the solution to deliver the goods and that hadn't transpired. We had some stories to tell but the primary objective of the mission hadn't been achieved. That said, it didn't take long to put the disappointment behind me. I love travelling on long haul flights, a glass of Sauvignon Blanc, a relaxing, dimly lit chair, a good book, what more could you ask for? I had stocked up in Ouray on reading material for the trip home. The local book shop had a long shelf of titles that were right up my alley. I had bought a few that I felt would get me though the 7-hour flight to Hawaii then 9-hr back to Australia. I sorted through the books in my carry bag and chose the one that I felt was best for this moment, "Rescues and Tragedies in the San Juan Mountains", by Kent Nelson. It was an exciting compilation of true stories that emphasised the risk of venturing into the Coloradan outdoors.

Through my work I had undertaken a speed-reading course that proved invaluable when digesting books such as these. I would generally begin reading at a relatively slow pace. If the subject matter gripped me I would continue at the slower pace, if the content was predictable and not so interesting, I would put the accelerator down and move rapidly through to the next chapter. In this case, while the content was exciting, it was also quite predictable. Adventurers driving of the side of cliffs, getting stuck high up in the mountains, being attacked by wild animals.

E. Pairing

A few hours into the flight, and a couple of glasses of Sauvignon Blanc for the better, I had hip-hopped my way to Chapter 17 – Where Are You? The fact the story was based around Ouray instantly grabbed my attention. Towards the bottom of the first page, it introduced the main characters of the story - Janice and Steve Okeson. My heart took a jump. My entire confidence in our solution was based upon the solving of the incredibly difficult "yew take Okeson Trailhead" clue. I had bet my annual bonus that Okeson Trailhead would lead us to the treasure.

Unbeknown to me Okeson Trail was named for an incident that occurred in 1977 and led to the biggest search in the county's history. "Where are you?" told the dramatic story of that incident.

Rather than plagiarise Kent Nelson's version from the book, I have rewritten the tragic story in verse below,

>Saturday morning, day was just dawning
>The mercury was falling fast
>Winter breathed hard, and bared her teeth
>Delivering a withering blast
>For this husband and wife, the rugged life
>Was a gritty and gruelling respite
>From the daily grind, they'd left behind
>To hunt at this rarefied height
>Their horses shivered, their bodies quivered
>High on the mountain trails
>They left their camp for the snow and the damp
>In search of elk in the vales
>Taking separate ways, through the timbered maze
>On either side of the ridge
>Hoping to bag a trophy stag
>Meat for the table and fridge
>Through winters curse, the storm got worse
>The trail disappeared from view
>On either side, of the mountain divide
>They struggled to find their way through
>He was first to have got, to the pre-arranged spot
>And waited for her to appear
>Seconds became minutes, and then turned to hours
>His disquiet turned to utter despair

The Pearl Necklace

He made a frantic search, amongst the alpine birch
In conditions increasingly dire
No trace was discovered, of his dearly beloved
His desperation grew higher and higher
Drawing on reserves, from adrenaline and nerves
He found his way back to the horses
Mounting his stead, he descended at speed
Driven by unknown forces
The dangerous drive down, to the box canyon town,
Was made without breaking or stops
He banged on the door, of Sherriff Lenore
And implored him to return to the tops
In fading light, they searched into the night
For signs of his missing love
No clue could be spied, as to the fate of his bride
It was as if she'd been plucked from above
His stamina spent, his resolve finally went
Steve collapsed in a heap in the snow
Tears cut a chase down his frost-bitten face
Melting holes in the blanket below
The next day awoke, so news of the loss
Drew searchers from towns far and near
In the worst weather of winter, they scoured the high hinter
For any sign of Janice, his dear
Still no signs could be found on the snow-covered ground
It was as Steve had first feared
Monday became Tuesday, then onto Wednesday
Then the weather finally cleared
The choppers flew in, with a thunderous din
Inspiration from the gun-metal sky
But the depth of the snow, in the valleys below
Kept hidden the snow butterfly
Thursday and Friday both came, the weather still tame
But the canyons gave up no clues
At the end of the week, the weather turned bleak
The Search and Rescue stood down their crews
With no signs to kindle, the numbers did dwindle
Soon Steve was searching alone

E. Pairing

> For the rest of the winter, he scoured the damn hinter
> Looking for his love to take home
> Spring brought respite, from winters cold bite
> The mountains of snow did thaw
> The rivers swelled from the alpine melt
> And thundered down to the valley floor
> Eventually the current, became less of a torrent
> And nature regenerated her beauty
> With seasons changed, another search was arranged
> By the Sheriff fulfilling his duty
> During a clear July week, they trekked up the creek
> And entered the vale from below
> And there in the rough at the base of the bluff
> Lay the body in quiet repose
> On a bright sunny day, they took her away
> From the flowers abundant there
> No longer alone, she took the long ride home
> Back to her families kind care

Reading the story in the dark at 30,000ft sent chills down my spine. I gazed across at Colt, Briar-Rose and Tyler sleeping comfortably to the hum of the plane's engines. I thanked God once again for delivering us safely back from our adventure. I knew they were going to be blown away by this story. The majestic grandeur of Winchester Gulch and its cascading waterfalls had disappeared behind a dark shadow. Had Fenn chosen this as the spot for his treasure due to this tragic past?

For the rest of the journey home, it was impossible to get the Janice Okeson tale out of my head. It brought a deeper, more mysterious aura to the chase. I was more convinced than ever that this was the spot Fenn had chosen for the chest and his final resting place. The next 12 months would be spent searching for clues to underline the accuracy of this hunch.

CHAPTER 9

CLOSER

Another good year at the factory and my resultant annual bonus provided the funds for another trip to recover the treasure. What was another $20,000 investment when there was a guaranteed $2M pot of gold at the end of the rainbow?

The 11 months between the trips had been spent collecting further evidence to support the Winchester Gulch theory, though to me it was no longer a theory, it was a dead-set certainty. Chapter 4 in TTOTC, "Jump -starting the learning curve," had provided the defining proof that this was the guaranteed solution. It tells a story of when Fenn was in seventh grade. His teacher a Miss Ford. At the time she was Fenn's favourite teacher. She was also the first clue in an elaborate story pointing the way to Winchester Gulch. When taking country road 14A up to Thistle Park there is a ford on the left-hand side. It takes you over Cutler Creek up to Storm Gulch. Miss Ford is an instruction to ignore the ford and go straight ahead across Thistle Park to Okeson Trailhead. This is underlined in the story when Fenn is sent to see his principal father, and the first thing his father says to him is "Okay son". The story finishes with Fenn boasting about sliding down a fire escape from his second storey class room to escape Spanish class. On the bottom of the last page is a picture of the Central Junior High School. The inscription under the picture relates that the fire escape is on the back of the building shown. However, if you look closely the school it has a number of downpipes that run from the second-floor guttering to the ground. If you extent these downpipes up the page into the title at the top

E. Pairing

of the page it spells out JANICE. The alignment isn't perfect, but close enough for me to spend $20,000 of hard-earned cash venturing back out into the Ouray County wilderness.

For this trip we chose to fly to LA then on to Denver, the drive being much shorter to Ouray than going via Las Vegas. There was no Grand Canyon or Monument Valley this time, it was just serious gold hunting business.

That was until we got to check-in at the airport.

"Sir, it appears your passport number doesn't match your ESTA."

"What does that mean," I queried as if the clerk was speaking another language.

"What it means sir, is you can't fly with us today unless you get a new ESTA issued."

"And how do I do that," I asked, the gravity of the situation starting to sink in.

"Your best bet would be at one of the travel agents in this building. They can apply for you, but I don't think you have got enough time to make this flight."

Colt, Briar-Rose, and Tyler stood there in utter disbelief. They were already safely cleared to board the flight and here was I having to make a mad dash against the odds to get on the same plane.

The next three hours were a blur. At the end of it, Colt, BR, and Tyler were jetting to LA, and I was sitting in the departure lounge waiting to catch a flight leaving in 10 hours to San Fransisco. Due to transposing two digits on the original ESTA application I was also making another $2000 investment into the Forrest Fenn economic stimulus package.

Once aboard the flight, I had 12 hours alone in the air to contemplate my mistake. I eventually arrived in Denver 8 hours behind the rest of the crew. It was then my luck began to take a turn for the better. The sales guy at the car rental company was Indian and a massive cricket fan. He was also the master of the up sell. By the time I walked out of his depot we had spent an hour swapping cricketing yarns and I was driving a brand new black Cherokee Jeep. It was dusk in Denver, and I felt relieved to be driving into the city to be reunited with the team.

The reunion was more subdued than I had envisaged. I was ecstatic to have travelled alone half way around the globe and made it safely to the motel in Denver. When I knocked on their room door the rest of the team seemed just a little pissed that I had mucked up so badly and depleted the travel fund so majorly. We headed out to the local tavern, and over a few drinks all was forgiven.

Next day we headed south. Before getting to our destination of Ridgway we had a couple of small matters to attend to. The first was in Delta where we planned to pay our respects to Janice. We bought flowers locally then drove to her final resting place in the Delta cemetery. Ominously, a massive storm had rolled in as we passed through the cemetery gate. Rain started falling as we searched for the correct Row and Number. Parking the Cherokee, Briar-Rose and I proceeded on foot despite the fact we had no protection from the rain. The weather conditions were such, the other half of the team stayed inside the vehicle. Lightning began crashing all around us, to the extent we feared for our lives. Frantically we ran down the rows checking headstone to headstone in an effort to locate Janices grave. By the time we found the site we were drenched to the skin. The lightning continued to strike around us as we lay the flowers upon her grave. We took some quick photos to remember the emotional occasion then sprinted back to the jeep. Once back inside, we feverishly rummaged over the back seat for a towel to dry ourselves off. Taking out my phone, I opened the photos we had taken, to share the experience with those who hadn't been willing to brave the elements. It was only then we realised the impact the loss of Janice had had on her family. Janice's gravestone was intentionally imbedded in the ground. It had a wilderness scene engraved across the top of it. The words showed Janice had died aged 21 years old on the 6th of November 1977. This was already known to us so was no real surprise. However beside her were the gravestones of her mother and brother. Her mother had died just months after her death at the age of 42. In an even more sinister twist, her brother had died on the same day, years later, also aged 42. We contemplated this as we left the cemetery and continued our journey south.

Reaching Montrose 22 miles down the road, we pulled into the carpark of the huge Walmart store to stock up for the expedition. While I made a bee line for the outdoors area I lost my other three companions as they disappeared into the food department. We met back at the checkout. They were weighed down with boxes of Jam Tarts, Cheezies, and other sugar-filled delights. I had managed to find the lifesaving bear spray, 100 yards of abseiling rope, fishing line and hooks in case we had to pull the treasure out of a deep hole, and an axe, and a hoe. The last

E. Pairing

two items were of special significance. While they would be useful items up Winchester Gulch, the symbol of the CISCO gang was a crossed axe and hoe. This had derived from the many photos of Fenn holding either an axe or a hoe. I had always felt this was a non-to-subtle hint that the chase was a hoax. I never did figure whether this was a bluff, a double bluff, or even a triple bluff.

We had decided to stay in Ridgway, being convinced the treasure was in Winchester Gulch. The plan was to travel back up Cow Creek and enter the gulch from below. Our accommodation was high on the hills above Ridgway looking out to the Rocky Mountains and its many snow-capped peaks. It was a postcard perfect view, with humming birds in the foreground just to add to the magical scene.

Rather than repeat our misadventures of the previous year we had hired a mountain guide to take us in on his all-terrain vehicle. We met him at the park in Ridgway's main street the next morning. He was an affable character named Billy Bison. We explained the plan to him, even letting him in on the reason for heading up Winchester Gulch. He claimed to have only vague awareness of the Fenn story but was happy to be in on the adventure. It was great to be sitting in the back, wind in the hair, with someone else at the wheel. BB was confident his vehicle, with its 5 axles and 20 tyres, could get us to the desired coordinates on the map.

Our confidence in BB took a small dent when he raised concerns about the condition of the road heading into Cow Creek. From the previous year we knew this was pussy country compared to what lay ahead. On reaching Cow Creek we were taken aback. The volume of water in the creek was considerably greater than a year ago, being two foot deep in parts. BB was hyperventilating and shaking his head a lot.

A long discussion with BB, impressing on him how we had traversed the stream a year ago in a rental car, and that $2M of treasure awaited him up the valley finally got him to move gingerly forward, down the bank and into the water. BB shouldn't have worried. His Swiss-built Unimog rolled through the current with ease. Unfortunately, we were unaware the vehicles battery was positioned under the front passenger seat. As we emerged from the stream sparks began flying from under the seat and the Unimog ground to a halt. Billy Bison swore under his breathe then revealed to us the source of the issue.

While BB worked to dry out the battery terminals, we stood beside the vehicle reliving the nightmare that was Cow Creek the year before. We pointed out the route the trail took across the face of the bluffs up the valley to BB. The blood drained from his face but given the $1000 cash we had given him one hour earlier, he gave a brave smile and indicated he was ready to proceed. We climbed back aboard and fastened our seat belts.

As we crawled up the heavily rutted track above Cow Creek I reached down and unclicked my seat belt. If we were going to go over the side I wanted to be ready to jump clear of the vehicle. We passed the turnaround point from last year. In the Unimog, it didn't seem quite as scary as then, as the vehicle was more suited to the terrain, and the open nature of the craft gave us some chance of survival if it went over the edge. Once we were back out on the bluff face, the fear factor really kicked in. Looking around the Unimog I'm not sure who was the most petrified. BB was focused completely on negotiating the ruts and contours of the track, and keeping his asset on the path. Briar-Rose was crushing Tyler's hand as if it was her last day on earth. Tyler stared down at the floor praying to his own god. Colt was gazing out across the wide expanse toward Winchester Gulch. He had his Go-Pro strapped to his head over his "Make America Great Again" cap and was taking in the experience. Everyone was silent, measuring their lives up until this point.

By the grace of god, we survived this ordeal. We rolled down off the high point across the bluff and into a valley carrying Red Creek down into Cow Creek. It was nearly bereft of water but was heavily bouldered, making traversing it difficult. By now, BB was past worrying. It was as if he thought it was his last day on earth and he would accept God's fate as it arrived. He chose his route across the creek and worked his way into it. Suddenly the sparking from under the front seat erupted again and the vehicle stopped dead. The minimal water flow meant we were safe from being swept away but it was clear we wouldn't be going anywhere fast.

We had another conference with BB to agree on the best course of action. As we were only half a mile from Winchester Gulch it was decided we would don our packs and proceed on foot. BB would get the Unimog going again and park it on a spot directly across Cow Creek from the gulch. He would wait for us there until we returned with the treasure in 3 hours' time. If we hadn't returned by then he would wait another hour then return to town and raise the alarm. If he wasn't parked in the

E. Pairing

appropriate spot we would walk up the track to Red Creek. For BB it seemed a pretty good deal given we had cut him in for 10% of the treasure for acting as a guide to take us up Winchester Gulch.

The walk to Winchester Gulch was enjoyable. We encountered many of the wildlife delights that make the Colorado outdoors so remarkable. We even saw a young mule deer at close range. It seemed as stunned as we were to be at such close proximity. Some folks argue this is the real treasure in the Chase and it is hard to disagree.

Eventually the trail exited out onto the gravel maze that is Cow Creek. From here on our planned route was off trail with no paths or signposts. Even establishing which valley off Cow Creek was Winchester Gulch was open to question. After some debate we waded across the stream and entered the bush. It was primarily White Beech trees with heavy bush undergrowth covered in the red berries that had populated the bear skat we had encountered 12 months previous. It was steep and tiring given our level of fitness. After some searching we found a rock-strewn creek bed. Incredibly there was no sign of water flowing down it in spite of there being the roar of a large waterfall further up the valley. We fought our way up the creek bed climbing over and under fallen trees crossing the route. In time we came to water. It was flowing down from a small waterfall before disappearing under the rock bed we had been struggling up. Incredibly it continued this subterrain course all the way to Cow Creek where there was no obvious evidence of it joining the larger river.

The hiking was very strenuous forcing us to stop frequently to catch our breathe. At these times we would discuss our progress and check the time, as we had to find the site, recover the treasure, and return to Billy Bison within the 3-hour allotted time. This being the case we had allowed 2 hours to get to the site and find the chest, and one hour to return to the Unimog.

It was after about an hour we encountered our first major obstacle. We reached an impassable solid rock face 6 metres high with a small amount of water cascading over it. To the left of the wall was a vertical cliff face that couldn't be scaled without specialist equipment. To the right was an almost vertical scree face that rose several hundred feet before meeting another vertical cliff face. Up above the impassable waterfall we could see the distinct rock formations we had viewed many times on Google Earth. There were caves in the massive rock bluffs that

The Pearl Necklace

looked the ideal site for secreting $2M dollars-worth of treasure. Higher up the valley we could just make out the gigantic overhanging rock formation that fitted with many of Fenn's pictorial clues and lead us to believe the chest was deposited in this remote location.

Determined not to be beaten, we weighed our options. There was only two we could come up with. One, fell a tree onto the face of the waterfall and climb it to the top of the fall. Two, climb the scree face and make our way to the next level via that route. Rather than damage the environment we chose to go with option 2.

Surveying the scree face, we selected a route that would take us 100 feet up the bank then across and down onto the shelf above the waterfall. Colt and I started out side by side. It was tough going. Each step was carefully made to ensure we were going forward rather than slipping backwards on the shifting rock face. It also paid not to look down as the fall behind us became more perilous with each step. Being fitter, Colt gradually pulled away the higher we climbed. Taking care not to be directly below him, I stopped frequently to catch my breathe. He reached the desired height after about 20 minutes. I still had 30-odd feet to go, and had stopped for another rest, sitting on a football sized rock. Being conscious of the need to press on I hurriedly stood up from the rock, dislodging it in the process. The large rock moved slowly at first before rapidly gaining momentum down the steep scree slope. Tyler and Briar-Rose had started to scale the rock-strewn cliff, following the same route as Colt and I had taken.

By the time the run-away rock reached them it was hurtling directly toward BR. Colt yelled a warning causing her to look up just as the rock rocketed towards her head.

Like a mountain lion, Tyler dived sideways, tackling BR around the waist. The rock whistled past her face, avoiding a potentially fatal accident by inches.

With Tyler still clutching BR, they tumbled over the jagged rocks down the 20 feet they had scaled, into the creek bed below. Both had rips and tears to their clothing and blood seeping from cuts and abrasions on their arms and legs, but miraculously had escaped major injury.

It became immediately apparent our treasure hunting was over for the day. We were in awe of how Tyler had prevented what could have been a tragic disaster. The knowledge that we were in the same valley where Janice had lost her life was not lost on us. There was very little

E. Pairing

discussion over the best cause of action, we simply made sure everyone was capable of retracing our steps down the valley and began our descent back to Cow Creek.

Emerging from the bush we found BB lying on his back, totally naked beside the mountain stream. He had been bathing in the ice-cold water and was now happily drying himself off in the afternoon sun. Our crashing through the undergrowth occasioned him to open his eyes. With no drama or hurry, he nonchalantly reached for his clothes and started to dress.

"No treasure I see," he stated, as he pulled on his short-sleeved shirt over his partially wet body.

"I guess I'm going to have to keep working." He pulled on his shorts and proceeded to wade across Cow Creek toward the Unimog parked in the shade below the trees on the far side of the stream.

In stunned disbelief we followed suit, crossing the creek in a tight huddle.

The ride back to town was a rollercoaster of emotions. In that respect it was a replay of the year before. We had started out with such high expectations and were bitterly disappointed at not having reached our destination, while at the same time we were grateful not to have been seriously injured or killed in the process.

BB dropped us at the park in central Ridgway. It was late afternoon with the sun disappearing down behind the surrounding hills. After stashing our gear in the rental car BR, Tyler, and I headed across the road to the True Grit café. Colt was knackered and headed into the park to a seat in the shade under a large oak tree. As the name suggests, the True Grit Cafe is a trip back in time to the days when cowboys ruled this part of the country. Western memorabilia adorned every available space both inside and outside the establishment. To further enhance the scene the shop adjoining the café was a treasure trove of vintage Americana. Large red, white, and blue rosettes and bunting decorated the veranda along the row of shops containing the café. The Stars and Stripes fluttered in the breeze from poles on either side of the entrance.

Finding a table in the upstairs dining room we settled into a sumptuous feed of hamburgers, chips, and cold beer. Sitting amongst the other diners we cut a sorry sight. They were mainly neatly dresses family groups with young children. By contrast we were dirty and dishevelled, our clothes filthy and torn. Briar-Rose and Tyler still had batches of dried blood on their arms and weeping wounds about their knees. Our muscles ached and our bodies longed for a soft bed.

While the food and drink brought relief to the physical pain, the mental impact of our failure to reach the treasure site was becoming harder to recover from. The second near-to-tragedy experience was also weighing heavily on us. Looking out over the park in the town square we could see Colt sitting with BB in deep discussion about something, while we debated the sanity of venturing back up Winchester Gulch the following day. Although it was by no means unanimous, we agreed that returning to Winchester would be tempting fate, and we would instead take the opportunity to take in the spectacular sights in the surrounding area.

Exiting True Grit we made our way along the wooden veranda to the antique and collectables shop next door. Colt saw us leaving the café and crossed the road to join us. The shop was filled with glorious treasures. Just maybe we could find something to lessen the disappointment of not finding the real thing.

It was packed from floor to ceiling with memorabilia and knick-knacks from the old West. And there at the counter, in conversation with the owner, was the unmistakeable figure of Denim Belle. Although she had her back to us, her shapely outline and distinctive dress sense left no doubt we were once again in the company of our old friend.

I looked around to warn Colt of the impending encounter, but he had already taken evasive action, ducking across into the adjoining room of the store. Only then did I notice the white, old-style pram at Denim Belle's side. Until then it had blended in with the rest of the surroundings. Belle's hand rested on the ornate mother-of-pearl handle, and she gently moved it back and forward.

As I weighed my options she turned and caught sight of us.

"Aussies," she growled softly, moving toward us with outstretched arms. Not wanting to appear rude, I reached out and embraced her tightly. "Fancy seeing you again," she said warmly, her eyes shifting to the blue-eyed cherub looking up at us from the pram.

"Don't worry, it's not what you think. I'm minding him for my sister."

"That's what they all say," I countered.

A broad smile came across her face.

"Gotta run, I've got a long ride home," Belle responded as she scooped up her purchase and hustled past us and out the shop doors.

CHAPTER 10

WTF

March 2020. Covid had cast its long shadow over the earth, international borders had closed, and even interstate travel within countries had been curtailed. The 10th anniversary of the Chase was approaching, and the treasure was still out there. A new plan was needed, and a recent discovery sparked an idea in my mind.

I had been trying to unravel one of Fenn's convoluted stories, about a friend of his, Charmay, who had spent a lot of time with Fenn excavating relics in Taos. In cryptic language char could refer to tea (T), and May to the fifth month of the year (5). Far-fetched I know, but I was exploring all avenues. A quick search online for "T5 Ouray" brought up an abseiling course offered by the San Juan Mountain Guides (SJMG). Under Covid, the tourism industry in the USA had been devastated. Surely it would be a win-win situation if I could engage the mountain guides to go out and recover the treasure. In fact, why hadn't I thought of this idea earlier. It would have been way cheaper and much less dangerous.

An exchange of emails with the guides got an enthusiastic response. As expected, business was quiet, and they were struggling to generate any sort of revenue in these difficult times. They assigned a guide to me who had vast experience in the mountains around Ouray. As a bonus, the guide, Bindi-Anna, had a partner, Darion, who was also passionate about the great outdoors. They spent most of their free time in the mountains with their blue heelers Skull & Bones. Even better, Bindi-Anna and Darion were familiar with the Fenn Chase, and keen to help find the treasure.

Over the next few weeks, we agreed terms and an equitable split of the treasure when it was recovered. Numerous emails went back and forward explaining the Ouray solution, and the likely hiding place in Winchester Gulch. This process generated a high degree of excitement as information flowed back and forth. Finally, a timetable was agreed upon, and a communication plan put in place. Being professional mountain guides SJMG had the latest in GPS tracking and real-time feedback to customers.

Wednesday 8th April: First Expedition

The plan for the day was simple. Bindi & Darion would drive up to the meadow cum under-used campground beside Cutler Creek. They would then tramp up Okeson Trail to Baldy Ridge at 10800 feet, then descend down into Winchester Gulch, where the famed treasure would await them.

With the time difference between USA and Australia being 8 hours, Bindi and Darion were out on the trail when I awoke at 5am. Live updates from their trek up Okeson Trail toward Winchester Gulch were already in my inbox as I sat down to breakfast. It was a spectacular day in the hills above Ouray, with bright blue skies and crystal-clear visibility. Over my cornflakes I opened the live feed. Pictures were coming through showing a large cave they had found at the head of the valley above Cutler Creek. We were totally unaware of this caves existence as it wasn't shown on any maps, but its size and stand-out nature convinced Bindi and Darion it was important to the chase. It was lined with white marble and was visible from several kilometres away.

This was a major penny-drop moment. I scrambled for a map of the area. The coordinates from Bindi's GPS allowed me to plot their position and that of the cave on the map. The solution was obvious and highlighted two years of wasted effort. Winchester Gulch was not the end point of the chase! Winchester Gulch was, as its name suggested, a rifle imprinted on the landscape, with the lower reaches of the gulch forming the handle of the weapon, and the upper reaches the barrel of the gun. Drawing a line from the barrel of the gun, as if firing a bullet, the projectile would meet the site of the cave several kilometres away. This was very similar to the solution in the Edgar Allen Poe book The Gold Bug.

Communications with Bindi and Darion became frantic. Quit the plan to venture down into Winchester Gulch. Instead travel across from Okeson Trail and investigate the cave.

E. Pairing

It was hard to concentrate on the day-to-day issues of running a dairy factory once arriving at work. It was a busy day, with the usual production meetings and a monthly board meeting scheduled.

The production meetings came and went, then there was the board meeting to navigate. Sitting before the company directors, my boss, the CEO, read through his report. I couldn't help but look down at my phone and open the comms coming through from Bindi & Darion. They had ventured across to the cave and were exploring in and around it. Inside the cave they had discovered the nest of a pair of Golden Eagles. It was no simple bird's nest. The branches that made up the nest were as thick as your fingers, and the nest spanned several metres. Bindi, already familiar with Fenn's poem suggested the relevance of "if you are brave and in the woods". I wasn't convinced, but I was certain of the relevance of the cave to the Chase.

By now it was late afternoon in Ouray. Bindi & Darion had indicated they would camp in the vicinity of the cave and make their way back to Ouray in the morning. We could then digest the new information and formulate a new plan.

The work day couldn't finish soon enough. Once back at home I pulled out all the files pertaining to the possible connection to the marble cave. My mind was working overtime. How could I have been so naïve. Clearly the chase was longer and more elaborate than I originally envisaged. But my two years of late nights and intense research had prepared me for this moment. I was well founded in Fenn's stories relating to marble structures. He had concocted many stories relating to three marble constructions, the relevance of which up until now were a mystery. The structures, in no particular order were, the shower within his private den at his house in Santa Fe, the vault of the Skull & Bones fraternity at Yale in New Haven, and the Tomb of the Unknown Soldier in Arlington Cemetery in Washington DC. Interestingly but unconnected, the marble for that tomb also came from Colorado, quarried from Treasure Mountain. Apart from all being made from marble the 3 structures and the stories surrounding them shared similarities, one being that they all initially, and controversially, excluded women from entry. Fenn makes a number of references to New Moon in his writings. It just happens NEW MOON is an anagram for NO WOMEN.

The discovery of the Marble Cave meant there would be very little sleep that night. The inclusion of the cave in the chase was a master stroke by Fenn. Any searcher would have to be out in the field to discover it and recognise its significance to the hunt. Incredibly, by an amazing act of god it was situated on the bullet line from Winchester Gulch. The presence of the Golden Eagle's nest further verified the caves linkage to the hunt and the treasure, as the treasure chest was filled with Golden Eagle and Double Golden Eagle coins. In the poem there is the line "But tarry scant with marvel gaze." Is it possible MARVEL GAZE is a sound alike for MARBLE CAVE?

Before setting up camp for the night Bindi & Darion had thoroughly checked out the cave and the nest for any signs of the treasure. They took special care not to disturb the nest. Though it was not being occupied at the time, it was likely it would come back into service once the breeding season for the Golden Eagles resumed. It was no surprise that no treasure was found. Fenn that openly stated on numerous occasions, the treasure was hidden at an altitude of between 6000 and 10500 feet. The cave was at 10600 feet.

It was becoming apparent, with my fixation on Winchester Gulch I had overlooked an important aspect of the chase, being Fenn's assertion that there were 9 clues that would lead you to the treasure. The discovery of the cave was a light bulb moment that brought this home to me; the chase was a point-to-point treasure hunt where you had to solve the clues to move from one location to the next. This begged the question, what number site was the Marble Cave?

By my reckoning it was most probably No. 6

1. Begin it where warm waters halt = Ouray Hot Springs
2. The Home of brown = Ouray Waste Water Treatment Plant
3. The end is ever (I sever) = Cutler Creek
4. I SEEK, THE A(nswer) I ALREADY KNOW = YEW TAKE OKESON TRAILHEAD
5. hinT of RICHES NEW = WINCHESTER
6. Tarry Scant with marvel gaze = Black Spars(e) with Marble Cave
7. ??
8. ??
9. ??

Surely the secret to uncovering the last 3 clues lay in understanding the marble structures. Fenn had always said, "Imagination is more

E. Pairing

important than knowledge". Surely this was the case here. All I had to do was interpret what Fenn's shower, The Skull & Bones vault in New Haven, and the Tomb of the Unknown Soldier in Washington DC had to do with a Marble Cave at the head of a gully just outside of Ouray. I opened a bottle of Sauvignon Blanc, cut some cheese, and settled in for a long night.

A topographical map was spread out on the table before me. I studied it closely. The marble cave actually sat at the head of two valleys, each home to a creek that ran down its valley on either side of a rocky promontory before coming together and forming a single creek that then fed into Cutler Creek. On the map the creeks resembled deer antlers with almost perfect symmetry.

Relating this back to Fenn's bathroom, the taps in his marble shower could represent the source of the water for each of the creeks. I pondered this for a moment, sipping from the half-full wine glass.

Then it came to me like a bolt from the blue. In the TTOTC Fenn delivers up a mega clue on the final page of the book. He makes a rather bizarre statement about a butterfly really being a "flutterby". He then goes on to say something deep and meaningful about the past.

Past, the last word in the book. PAST is an anagram for TAPS! Anyone with a military background is familiar with Taps. It is a bugle call played at the funeral or at dawn for fallen soldier. Though typically just a musical rendition, there are lyrics to Taps. They are known as Butterfields Lullaby!

> Day is done, gone the sun,
> From the lake, from the hills, from the sky;
> All is well, safely rest, God is nigh.
>
> Fading light, dims the sight,
> And a star gems the sky, gleaming bright.
> From afar, **drawing nigh**, falls the night.
>
> Thanks and praise, for our days,
> 'Neath the sun, 'neath the stars, neath the sky;
> As we go, this we know, God is nigh.

Sun has set, shadows come,
Time has fled, Scouts must go to their beds
Always true to the promise that they made.

While the light fades from sight,
And the stars gleaming rays softly send,
To thy hands we our souls, Lord, commend.

It describes the end of the day, analogous to the passing of the serviceman. There is a clear linkage between the lyrics to Taps and Fenn's poem. On line 6 Butterfield uses the turn of phrase, drawing nigh, as does Fenn on Line 10 of his poem.

All this ties in nicely with the Tomb of the Unknown Soldier in Arlington Cemetery, Washington DC. But for the grace of God, Forrest Fenn could have ended up as the Unknown Soldier. He was shot down in Vietnam. Having survived the crash, he was winched from the dense forest under enemy fire to be miraculously returned safely to his family in the States.

Fenn often said, 'find the Blaze and you will find the treasure'. Most searchers were looking for physical aspects like rock scars, or scarfs cut in trees to fulfil this edict, however in this case it turns out the Blaze was a person.

The original Unknown Soldier for the Vietnam War was Michael Blassie, someone Fenn would have definitely known. He was a fellow fighter pilot about the same age as Fenn. His Dragonfly fighter jet was shot down in Vietnamese jungle, a crash he didn't survive. His nickname **"The Blaze"**.

Much controversy surrounds the selection of Blassies body to be the Unknown Soldier. There was suspicion that the body found in the Vietnamese jungle was Blassie's. Despite this suspicion the military went ahead with the use of the remains as the Unknown Soldier. However, they didn't bank on the tenacity of another Vietnam Vet Ted Sampley whose continued investigation of the story lead to DNA evidence proving the remains were indeed Blassies. Amidst great controversy the body was exhumed from the Tomb of the Unknown Soldier and took the long ride home back to Blassies home state of Missouri to be re-interred.

E. Pairing

So apart from Taps what was the significance of the Tomb of the Unknown Soldier to the chase? My suspicion was the need to overlay a map of Arlington Cemetery over the valleys below the cave. The cemetery has many prominent features, including the gravesite of John F Kennedy, Joe Louis the brown bomber, and other notable Americans. It is likely one of these features would coincide with one of the physical features in the valleys, and there would be the treasure.

It took several nights, and several bottles of fine pinot, to crack the significance of Arlington, but the discovery was worth waiting for. When it happened, it opened a waterfall of enlightenment. Staring at a map of the national cemetery it became clear there were numerous small loop roads within the precinct. What if we placed one of these rings over the delta of the creeks running down the valleys? Eureka, this was the ultimate lightbulb moment. By placing a circle around the Y delta, it forms the Mercedes Benz symbol. This seemingly simple action precipitated an avalanche of realisation. It was as if we had found the Rosetta Stone to the Fenn treasure hunt. The final pieces of the puzzle all fell into place and the hunt was complete.

The Mercedes Star is mentioned obliquely in the poem in line 17, "So why is it that I must go?". Intentionally inserted to falsely point solvers at the John Muir quote, "the mountains are calling, so I must go", it actually references the John Masefield poem Sea Fever, "I must go down to the sea again, to the lonely sea, and the sky……..". The 3-pointed Mercedes Star was designed to represent Land, Sea, and Air.

While this is all very interesting, the circle around the delta could just as easily represent the peace sign from the 60s and 70s, or the telescopic sight on a rifle. Well, it does, but for now the Mercedes Star provides a vital clue into the final three outstanding locations in the chase. To find the clue purely through the "I must go' reference would have been virtually impossible, so Fenn gives out a major clue in the foreword to OUAW, where he introduces Lynda Obst. Reading through her Wikipedia profile we find she worked extensively on the movie 'The Fisher King'. One of the stars of the film is the actress Mercedes Ruehl.

This was a major revelation. One of the overarching themes of the chase is the movies of Jeff Bridges. Fenn manages to knit a wide selection of these films into the Chase. However, at this point it is the Fisher King that is the vital link. It is not the movie itself that is relevant, but the legend of the Fisher King. It is the story of one of the greatest quests in history – the search for the Holy Grail!

In Arthurian legend, the Fisher King, also known as the Wounded King or Maimed King, is the last in a long bloodline charged with guarding the Holy Grail. Versions of the original story vary widely, but the king is always wounded in the legs or groin and incapable of standing. All he is able to do is fish in a small boat on the river near his castle, Corbenic, and wait for some noble who might be able to heal him by asking a certain question. In later versions, knights travel from many lands to try to heal the Fisher King, but only the chosen one can accomplish the feat.

The injury is a common theme in the telling of the Grail Quest. The wound is sometimes presented as a punishment, usually for philandering. In the medieval romantic poem *Parzival*, the king is injured by the bleeding lance as punishment for taking a wife, which was against the code of the "Grail Guardians". In some early story lines, Percival asking the Fisher King the healing question cures the wound. The nature of the question differs between *Percival* and *Parzival*, but the central theme is that the Fisher King can be healed only if Percival asks "the question".

The location of the wound is of great importance to the legend. In most medieval stories, the mention of a wound in the groin or more commonly the "thigh" is a euphemism for the physical loss of or grave injury to one's penis. In medieval times, acknowledging the actual type of wound was considered to rob a man of his dignity, thus the use of the substitute terms "groin" or "thigh", although any informed medieval listener or reader would have known exactly the real nature of the wound. Such a wound was considered worse than actual death because it signalled the end of a man's ability to function in his primary purpose: to propagate his line. In the instance of the Fisher King, the wound negates his ability to honor his sacred charge.

E. Pairing

Just above the delta of the creeks down the valleys below the cave lies a large rock formation. Surely this represented Castle Rock or Corbenic. Another look at the poem, another glass of red, and this theory was verified.

LOOK QUICKY DOWN / Y / OUR QUEST / TO CEASE

In the crossword world LOOK QUICKLY is to peek. In cryptic crossword speak, DOWN is to reverse the word i.e. peek becomes keep. A keep is a castle.

The Y represent the delta of the two creeks

Our quest we will get to shortly.

To cease is generally accepted as referring to two C's. This could refer to Cutler Creek, but more likely Corbenic, which starts and finishes with the letter in question.

Going back to OUR QUEST the answer is pure genius and has probably baffled most searchers ever since OUAW was published. What is the significance of the stickman with the turquoise belt buckle? Here is the stunning revelation. The stick man is a map of the final area, his legs forming the delta of the two creeks, his body the combined creek, his arms Cutler Creek that the combined creek joins not far below the delta. OUR QUEST is an anagram for TURQUO(I)SE. The turquoise buckle is a map of the area at the delta, complete with the minute gold square representing the chest, and a small orange square.

The small orange square represents the delta with the circle around it. The word orange can be separated into O RANGE that translates to O SCOPE, describing the symbol as a rifle scope. This provides a datum point on the buckle map to then establish where the treasure chest is hidden. The exactness of the solution had narrowed the search area to a relatively small area of ground of less than 50 square metres.

Emotions were now off the scale. Both the CISCO team and B&D were briefed on the solution. There was supreme confidence in its potential. No time was to be lost. It was agreed, B&D, together with Skull & Bones, would venture back up Cutler Creek tomorrow and retrieve the treasure.

Tuesday 14th April 2020 - Second Expedition

The timing of the treasure's retrieval was scheduled so the CISCO team could witness the event first hand. We gathered in the war room, comfortably lounging on the leather couches in front of the 60"inch screen. Colt took care of the technology, connecting the screen via his phone to B&D's satellite phone in the field.

After a couple of dial rings, the screen came to life. The immediate scene was familiar to the CISCO crew. It was coming via a headcam from the back of a ute traveling up a narrow gravel trail. We immediately recognised it as the track up Country Road 14A to the meadow by Cutler Creek. The camera turned and Bindi's face came into view. She was sitting on the back of the ute with her back to the cab. Skull & Bones were tucked in beside her, their tongues hanging out, taking in the mountain air.

"Hi guys," she shouted over the roaring engine, "Today's the day," she added, giving us a wide smile and a peace sign.

"Looking good," we offered back, "Wish we were there."

"Not the greatest of days," Darion growled, turning the headcam to sky. "Looks like we may get a wet butt."

The sky was grey and ominous.

"OK, we'll come back to you once we are up at the trail, probably 20 min by the time we get organised."

"All good," we chipped in, "'Take care."

The screen flashed off and we were left sitting in semi-darkness.

"Take care alright," BR said to herself, "The ride up that track scared the beejeebers out of me."

The suspense was now palpable. This was it. Within the next couple of hours, we were to become the finders of the famed Fenn treasure. It dawned on me we really didn't have a plan. We had agreed with B&D on the distribution of the loot, and a no publicity period, but nothing beyond that.

The next twenty minutes took forever, but it was a very pleasant forever. There was a warm smugness in the room. Thoughts were clearly passing through everyone's minds like those when you imagine winning the lottery. New car, a holiday, a boat, anything but work.

Finally the phone rang, and the screen sprang back to life. Bindi was posing beside a signpost, pack on with walking poles in hand. Skull and

E. Pairing

Bones were circling her feet, rearing to go. The sign was dilapidated and barely readable in parts, but Okeson Trailhead was still visible.

"Getting closer folks," Bindi exclaimed enthusiastically. "Heading up Cutler Creek from here. We'll leave the camera on. You'll see it as we see it."

"Look out for the bears," BR warned.

"Not a problem for this team," Bindi replied, giving a thumbs up, before turning and heading off toward the creek bed.

The water flow was minimal as they trekked up Cutler Creek. It was a couple of yards wide at its widest and only a couple of inches deep at its deepest. It appeared easier to walk up the creek bed rather than on the banks, as there was much debris and snow fallen trees accumulated there. The trek up the creek was picturesque without being spectacular. The gain in altitude was only slight and it was easy to imagine an eighty-year-old man taking this route.

After about ten minutes of hiking, Bindi stopped and consulted her GPS. Darion and her came together and there was a discussion going on regarding a small water source entering into Cutler Creek. Bindi turned and addressed the headcam. "Not our side creek", Bindi advised. "This one follows Okeson Trail up the valley. Ours should be about another 100 yards further on. Gotta tell ya, I'm feeling Forrest is with us today, feeling good vibes". With that she turned and carried on up the creek bed, in pursuit of Skull and Bones who were splashing their way forward up ahead.

Another 5 mins and the scene repeated. A small water source entering from the same side as the last. Like the last, it was fairly non-discreet, barely a foot wide with limited flow.

"This is it," declared Bindi, consulting her GPS again, "Getting close now."

Progress was slower now. The side creek was much narrower and the banks a little steeper. The debris and tree snow damage were more intense. I gazed around the war room. The CISCO crew were on the edge of their seats. The prospect of instant riches had overcome them. They were firmly in the grip of Fenn fever.

Before long Darion and Bindi arrived at the delta. It was not as I had imagined. It was hard to define and ugly to say the least. Two nondescript trickles of water came together and formed the creek up which we had just trekked. Up ahead you could vaguely make out the Castle Rock although it was largely hidden by a tangled mess of healthy and fallen birch trees.

The Pearl Necklace

According to the turquoise buckle, the treasure was level with the delta, most likely to the east if the stickman was to be true to form. B&D had been briefed on this and headed off into the shambles in that direction.

Progress was even slower now. The banks of the creek were an almost impassable tangle of fallen timber. Skull and Bones had minimal trouble jumping through the undergrown, but the same couldn't be said for B&D. Straddling the downed logs or burrowing under them was a near impossible mission.

It was theorised the treasure could possibly be 39 steps from the delta. This was based upon the fetish necklace placed within the treasure chest, a clear reference to the literary classic, The 39 Steps.

Skull and Bones were the first to spot the item sitting under the tangled debacle of logs. They began barking wildly as if cornering a wild pig. B&D hastened their efforts to navigate the labyrinth and find the source of the commotion. The headcam beamed live footage to the other side of the planet as this chaos ensued. Jerky pictures illuminated the screen in the war room. Suddenly an amazingly sight can into view. Two blue heelers, heads down, rummaging at a square metal box, sitting on the ground beneath a criss-cross of white birch debris.

The war room erupted into a scene of delirium. BR & Tyler hugged wildly. Colt looked across and gave me an unrestrained fist pump.

"Yes," shouted Bindi, "We've found it." She dived down and scurried under the logs to the chest.

"What the fuck."

Bindi's outburst quelled the exuberance instantly. All eyes reverted back to the screen. By now Darion was much closer to the chest. It became immediately clear, while the item was the same size as the Fenn chest, it was not an ornate Romanesque chest, but a rusty old camp oven.

It was as if someone had poured a bucket of cold water on a roaring fire. Total misbelief came over the collective group. In the exact spot predicted in the solution there was a rusty old camp oven, the same size and dimensions as the treasure chest.

"Now that's a surprise," I offered, trying to lighten the atmosphere.

The next ½ hour became a blur. The CISCO crew unravelled to other rooms in the house, and I made polite goodbyes to B&D in Colorado, promising to reconnect in the next few days.

CHAPTER 11

FULL CIRCLE

It took hours, if not days, to comprehend what had transpired that morning. Initially it was easiest to pass off what had occurred as a remarkable coincidence, however, given the confidence in the solution, and the exactness of the location, it was difficult to accept this position.

Over the next few weeks, the enthusiasm drained out of the team. What was Fenn up to? Surely the camp oven must have been placed by him and be part of the overall plan. We were now at a dead end and had no ideas as to the path to take next.

I can't remember the exact circumstances under how it came to me, but it did. It wasn't a new way forward, but it was further evidence the camp oven was planted by Fenn. I think I was lying in bed at the time, scrolling through the 9 clues to the treasure in my head and it suddenly dawned on me, the answer to each of the clues started with an O or a C or both. And those that didn't, like Winchester, could be pictorially represented by an O i.e. the end of the barrel. The Camp Oven was a continuation of that trend, and as such was a bit of a joke by Fenn. It didn't help that the Camp Oven was the same dimensions as the treasure chest, and when the lid is lifted the element is a perfect circle.

1. Ouray
2. Waste water treatment plant – the two ponds formed two O's when viewed on a map
3. Cutler Creek
4. Okeson Trailhead

5. Winchester Gulch – the end of the barrel represents an O or OO depending on whether it is single or double barrelled
6. Marble Cave – the cave is an O plus marbles are that shape, as in a number of Fenn's stories about marbles
7. Castle Rock & Corbenic
8. Mercedes Star
9. The Camp Oven

Given the item that took us to "the treasure" was the turquoise buckle, just maybe the overall path to the hunt represents the rest of the belt, and the clues are the holes in the belt. The O's are the perfectly formed holes and the C's less perfect holes.

Looking quickly back at the poem we see "Begin it where warm waters halt". The first two letters of the line are BE and the last two letters are LT, forming the word BELT. Is this just another coincidence?

Extending this idea out, maybe, like a belt, the hunt is circular and ends up back where it starts. Now I was getting excited again. Perhaps this was the way forward.

When first venturing up the treacherous gravel road to Cutler Creek, beside the track is the old wooden tower. It stands high above the trail, dark and foreboding, with no obvious purpose. What if that was the end point to the Chase. Fenn finishes the last sentence in each chapter of TTOTC with a small dark square, exactly how the tower was identified on the map of the area.

Then something else dawned on me. What if the Mercedes Star pointed at the tower. Grabbing the map I spread it over the table in the war room. Finding the delta of the two creek and ruling a line from the joint creek it was definitely heading in the right direction toward the tower. Sure enough, the line perfectly met the tower 2 miles away. But what was the significance of this revelation?

A fine bottle of Pinot Noir to celebrate the find, and some nice Australian cheese, and the puzzles pieces began to rapidly fall into place. The end of the hunt had been based upon arguably the greatest quest in history – the search for the Holy Grail. There is another quest story that is a more modern creation – the Dark Tower saga. Fenn uses Stephen King references throughout the Chase, starting with IT in the poem. It is highly likely Fenn knows King, being authors from neighbouring states, and appearing on book award lists together. This all forms the basis for much mystery and intrigue that will be explored later, but for now we are focussed on the Dark Tower series, King's opus magnus. The central character is Roland Deschain, the gunslinger, the last of a long lineage. He is on a quest to find the Dark Tower and has a mysterious enemy, known only as the Man in Black. The saga is written over 8 books and a short story, and draws inspiration from many sources, such The Lord of the Rings, Arthurian legend, Tolkien, and famous westerns like The Good, The Bad and the Ugly. Deschain's name and further inspiration for the series comes from the Robert Browning poem, "Childe Roland to the Dark Tower Came".

The Man in Black reference ties together a number of loose threads from Fenn's books. In many of his stories he meets women late at night, then again the next morning, but no impropriety occurs. This is the theme of the song "I walk the line" by the original man in black – Johnny Cash. Is this a hint or direction for us to follow the line drawn on the map from the delta to the dark tower? Could the treasure be hidden along this line? The countryside the line traverses is certainly hidden away enough to prevent the treasure from being stumbled across by chance, but still very accessible, ideal for an 80-year-old man looking to stow his chest and lay down and die.

The news went back out to the team, and to Bindi and Darion, the chase was back on. Somewhere along a 2-mile stretch of countryside the treasure was possibly hidden or buried.

The idea that Fenn may have buried the treasure bought a whole new dimension to identifying the precise spot where the loot was secreted. For some time, I had harboured a theory that you may have to go at night and retrieve the chest. Fenn could have used UV markers to identify the exact spot, and these could only be seen at night using a UV torch. Up until now I hadn't raised this with B&D as it is scary enough venturing out in the Coloradan wilderness during the day, let alone at night.

The UV light theory had been strengthened greatly when late one night I found Sir John Lubbock. Fenn had done much of his fighter pilot training in Lubbock, Texas. The naming of that town has nothing to do with Sir John Lubbock, but once you read Sir John Lubbock's biography you just know he must be linked to the chase. The salient points from his life history are:

- He was an English banker, politician, philanthropist, scientist, and polymath

- He was the 1st Baron of Avebury
- He made significant contributions in archaeology, ethnography, and several branches of biology. He coined the terms "Palaeolithic" and "Neolithic" to denote the Old and New Stone Ages, respectively.
- He helped found the X club, an elite group of the 9 most learned men in England, including Sir Charles Darwin, who met monthly for dinner and discussions.
- He discovered ants navigate by using UV vison. This enables them to move around at night.
- He bought land to help save a stone circle in Avebury, the largest in England.

If we go back to the poem, there are two aspects that could point to Lubbock and his interests. In line 15 we find "tarry scant with marvel gaze" which incorporates the phrase ANT WITH MARVEL GAZE. This could be a reference to the UV vision exhibited by ants.

Then in Line 23 we find "If you are brave......". It just happens that YOU + BRAVE = O AVEBURY.

Convincing B&D to go back out into the bush at night wasn't difficult. They spent many nights of the year camping out overnight, so this suggestion was nothing new to them. However, sourcing a UV torch during Covid proved to be a little more problematic. They looked in the local stores to no avail.

I tried to source one on-line, but delays and other issues made the procurement of the item difficult.

And then it happened.

CHAPTER 12

REST IN PEACE

The cell phone pinged on the bedside table. I rolled over and fumbled in the dark for my reading glasses.

Tapping the screen, it lit up displaying a text message. It was Bindi.

"Earl, I am so sorry. The treasure has been found!"

I rolled back over and tried to go back to sleep.

Why was Bindi sorry? I was fully expecting the treasure to be found. The 10-year anniversary of Fenn hiding the treasure had just passed. He had weathered the storm of controversy demanding the chase be called off following the deaths of 5 different searchers. Then the crazies had started to appear, taking out lawsuits against him, or threatening to kidnap his grandchildren. His health was failing, and he had withdrawn from making public appearances and comment. Rumours had been circulating for some time that he was keen to bring the chase to a close.

Morning came. Unfortunately, the news of the treasure's discovery had only brought further controversy. Both the identity of the finder and the location were being kept secret. On-line feedback was largely positive, with fellow searchers posting congratulatory messages. There was however an undercurrent of discontent. Where was the solution? How had the mystery finder managed to achieve what had baffled thousands of others for over 10 years?

This continued for a week then a media release was issued by the finder. Due to court action being taken out he had had to reveal his identity. He was a medical student from out east – Jack Stuef.

As for the solution, the finder, as he called himself, could only offer a rather contrived story. It centred around him working out where Fenn wished to die, then searching there for 25 days until he found the treasure. He threw in some weird details about following a diagram on a plastic bag and there being two search areas. He also added he had been driving to his desired search location but had been turned around by the snow. Only then did he find the final area. This was all rather unconvincing.

After several weeks of relentless pressure, the finder confided he had found the treasure in Wyoming. He also released an eloquent 3000-word letter. Here is a copy in its entirety:

My friend Forrest Burke Fenn passed away at the age of 90 earlier this month, and if I have anything to say about it, far too soon.

September 8 was certainly not the first time Forrest made me cry.

I am the person who found Forrest's famed treasure. The moment it happened was not the triumphant Hollywood ending some surely envisioned; it just felt like I had just survived something and was fortunate to come out the other end. For so long, I thought I might be haunted for the rest of my days by knowing where the treasure was but being unable to find it. Would I still be out there in that section of forest 50 years from now looking for it? When I finally found it, the primary emotion was not joy but rather the most profound feeling of relief in my entire life.

I figured out the location where he wished to die (and thus, where his treasure was) back in 2018, but it took me many months to figure out the exact spot. This treasure hunt was the most frustrating experience of my life. There were a few times when I, exhausted, covered in scratches and bites and sweat and pine pitch, and nearing the end of my day's water supply, sat down on a downed tree and just cried alone in the woods in sheer frustration.

I spent about 25 full days of failure looking for the treasure at that location before getting it.

When I got back to my rental car after the find, I put my hands on the steering wheel and bawled my eyes out. Then I remembered Forrest said the person who found the chest would either laugh out loud or start crying.

I realized he had been right and started to get annoyed that I still couldn't stop his quotes from popping into my head even after the chase was finally done.

E. Pairing

I laughed at myself for getting annoyed. Then I realized I had just fulfilled his other premonition about laughing out loud.

The treasure, a couple of feet from the nook in which it had been placed

In the weeks after, I still couldn't stop myself from reflexively thinking about what he was thinking. After living inside his head for two years, meeting him in person was sensory overload. I could now analyze his words and facial expressions and tone in real time, mere feet away from me. I could ask him questions about the chase and he would actually answer them! I never got used to it, and I was still analyzing him unnecessarily when he died, unable to turn my obsession off.

Now that he's gone, I'm no longer annoyed those Fenn quotes are still rattling around my brain. His words will live with me and every searcher out there for the rest of our lives.

I spent a couple more days crying after Forrest passed. He had meant so much to me in such a short time, and I had so much more I had wanted to ask him, the kind of things that were just better done face to face. For weeks he had wanted to fly me back to Santa Fe to spend more time with him (he even tried to convince me to move there), but circumstances out of our control made it more practical for me to come later.

I had never met Forrest until this June, and it was destined to be our only time spent together in person.

But I'm thankful for the time we did have. When I met Forrest, I told him I hadn't been sure I would ever get to meet him. The treasure was just too hard to find. He told me with a big smile that he had always said it was difficult to find but not impossible, and I had proved him right.

Forrest Fenn was born in 1930 in Temple, Texas. A poor student who disappointed his educator father, he grew into a life of adventure — a decorated Air Force pilot who was shot down in the Vietnam War and survived the Laos jungle, a rakish and prominent art dealer who courted the rich and famous, and, in his third and final act, a compulsive memoirist who wrote a poem that launched a treasure hunt in the Rocky Mountains that inspired many thousands of regular folks the world over.

The first line of his New York Times obituary calls him "eccentric." "I've been called 'eccentric' and I'm flattered by that," Forrest once said, "because the difference between an eccentric and a kook is an eccentric has money."

Forrest Fenn was the kind of man to drink buttermilk out of the bottle. He kept alligators in the garden of his art gallery. He collected run-over soda cans as pieces of found art. He loved books and language and held onto words like "crean" that apparently nobody but he still used. He went into business with former Texas Governor John Connally, the Johnson and Nixon confidante who was wounded by the "Magic Bullet" in the Kennedy assassination, to sell Elmyr de Hory's famed fraudulent masterpieces as fraudulent masterpieces. Forrest once shot a mountain lion and leapt down into a canyon, grabbed hold of the top of a tree, climbed down it, and tied the carcass to a rope so he could lift it out and get a $50 bounty from the Cattleman's Association.

He was also a man with an independent mind and a security with his masculinity (perhaps uncommon to those of his generation) that allowed him to express difficult feelings and question his own decisions and values in life, becoming a pacifist after retiring from the military and even regretting that affair with the beautiful mountain lion that had run in his direction.

Forrest wrote poignantly about his struggles with self-esteem and self-worth, and it's probably these writings I connected to most.

In the few years before I had heard of Forrest Fenn, my confidence in myself had been totally destroyed. I like to think it aided me in finding the treasure — without any self-confidence in my abilities, I had to stick to the evidence and not stray into hunches and speculation not strictly supported by the facts, and into their close cousin, confirmation bias.

Knowing the exact spot on the globe where a person would like to die is a weird intimacy to share with a stranger, but the experience of figuring it out and proving it beyond a reasonable doubt provided confidence that was intoxicating to me, and perhaps helping me regain that belief in myself will be Forrest's greatest legacy to me. In the outpouring of love Forrest received from his fans after his death, it was clear he knew just what to say to make people feel special. For me, it was soon after I told him I found the treasure, when he let me know, completely unprompted, that he thought I was a genius.

Few human beings peak as octogenarians. For most, old age is a slow dimming of the light, but Forrest fought against that. At 80, he attracted a large audience for the first time in his writing career, and in the next decade, as he continually dealt with the passing of his peers, he made hundreds or perhaps thousands of new friends, treasure searchers he met at gatherings and sometimes in his comfortable museum of a home.

For a decade, he wrote memoir at a breakneck pace, sharing the stories of his life with great relish yet seeming to never run out of them, even when he was down to telling us about the condiments in his refrigerator and the spices in his cabinets. He didn't seem to mind that much of his audience wasn't really listening to what he was saying and were only looking for secret hints.

For a man who expressed anxiety about getting Alzheimer's, he seemed to have found the perfect deterrent to cognitive decline — talking frequently and in guarded detail about a huge, closely-held secret to a cache of gold, yet never divulging it to the thousands of interested people inquiring. In a decade, he never made more than a couple of subtle slip-ups in front of all the dogged reporters who came to his house, and even those apparently haven't been caught by anyone besides me. He never paid to advertise his hunt, yet seemingly every media outlet wanted a piece of him, and he still managed to stay sharp as a tack and "keep his secret where" till the very end.

Forrest had the ultimate poker face. In the summer of 2018, the only time I had talked to Forrest on the phone before finding the treasure, I called to tell him in desperation I had found a "blaze" — the mark that the poem says points to the treasure — that seemed after some effort by me to have been faked by a cruel fellow searcher even though it had evidently been there for years. I couldn't believe the chances. I told him exactly where I had been searching, but the call only lasted about 20 seconds, and he gave no impression he found my discovery at all interesting.

That fake blaze was less than 1,000 feet from where I eventually found the treasure. And that's not even the half of that story.

When I met Forrest, he had forgotten about the phone call and found it amusing when I told him. Of course, he had no idea how much I had tortured myself trying to read his reaction to that call.

Lost in some of the remembrances of Forrest is his generosity. Forrest used his chase not for personal profit, but supported a local independent bookseller and raised tens of thousands of dollars for cancer victims. He was a benefactor and donated artifacts from his personal collection over the years to the Buffalo Bill Center of the West in Cody, Wyoming, on whose board he served for several years. Despite his years of disagreements with academics over the subject of archaeology, he supported and served on the board of the George C. Frison Institute at the Department of Anthropology at the University of Wyoming. Dr. Frison passed away the very same day as Forrest.

Of course, Forrest's greatest gift to humanity was his treasure. Sure, it could only be given to one person, the one who found it, but it inspired hope the world over and the joy of discovery for all those who got to go out and appreciate the wonders of the Rockies. No good deed goes unpunished, of course, and that hope spun off into myriad permutations Forrest couldn't have anticipated.

In some, that hope turned into false certainty in some people's minds, and they had to be rescued or tragically perished after finding themselves in dangerous circumstances out in the wilderness. In others, that hope turned into entitlement, that the hard work they put into this all-or-nothing hunt meant they were owed the treasure in some way, and that entitlement turned into bitterness and loud recitations of his personal imperfections that some declared to the world in the wake of his death. In others still, the hope turned into obsession that tricked their own minds into strange and harmful ideas. At my most raw points of gnawing frustration, even I resented Forrest.

Forrest had a tremendous penchant, though, for turning the other cheek. He did an incredible thing and dealt with tremendous doubt directed his way, but he kept to his word, and it was a gratifying experience to prove him right.

In a final act of selflessness, in what should have been his moment of redemption, he went to great lengths to protect my anonymity. Over the past decade, he and his family have suffered stalkers, break-ins, and a potential kidnapping (just to name the things that have been publicized) from misguided searchers. I told him I didn't want to be looking over my shoulder for people like that for the rest of my life, and he was completely understanding. Forrest went out of his way to protect me, a person he had never met before, even though in some ways it undermined the legitimacy of this hunt in some people's minds.

My family and I will be eternally grateful. It's incredibly generous to leave a chest full of gold out in the wilderness for someone to find. It's a whole other thing to set aside one's driving desire for a legacy in order to protect that stranger. Selflessness is the only way to describe it.

When I visited Forrest's house in June, he asked me if I had ever read his book on his friendship with the artist Eric Sloane, *Seventeen Dollars*

E. Pairing

a Square Inch. I hadn't. He gave me a copy. It's a classic Forrest Fenn production: lavish, large, very personal, a little eccentric, and totally indifferent to appealing to the book-buying public's wallets. But of course it looks gorgeous on my coffee table.

Getting the bracelet back and showing it off once again. The way his face lit up was indescribable. (Well, I was going to use the word "iridescent" to describe it just now, but for some reason a voice came into my head telling me to Google its definition in case I didn't know what it truly meant, and — yeah.)

In the craziness of the past few months, I neglected to read it, but I picked it up after Forrest passed, and I'm glad I did. It's a loving tribute of one friend to another, and reading it has helped me with my own loss. Its dust cover says:

Eric was a gifted painter and writer, and Forrest was a grateful admirer who sold his work. Their friendship lasted only ten years, but they were very influential years. You will see.

According to page 92, Forrest and Eric are busy now working to finish the book they began together years ago, so he won't notice if I steal and rework that passage:

Forrest was a gifted adventurer and writer, and the finder was a grateful admirer who sold his famous treasure. Their friendship lasted only three months, but they were very influential months. You will see.

Alas, I'm a millennial and have student loans to pay off, so it wouldn't be prudent to continue to own the Fenn Treasure. And at the end of the day, for all our similarities, Forrest and I couldn't be less alike when it comes to collecting. I'm the kind of person who feels burdened by possessions and most free adventuring the world out of a carry-on suitcase, so the treasure and I will have to soon part, and I will offer it for sale (minus the turquoise row bracelet returned to Forrest, of course).

The treasure is a unique piece of American cultural history. The gold glitters, but brighter still are the embedded hopes and dreams of all the many thousands who searched for it. It should belong to a person or institution who will fully appreciate owning such an incredible thing.

But Forrest had a final wish for where he thought the treasure should end up. The first step for me will be to try to make that happen.

As for the legacy of Forrest's chase, I suppose it is in many ways in my hands, as wrong as that feels. To be honest, I'm not sure what to do.

The Pearl Necklace

Whatever. Making plans is antagonistic to freedom. You will see. I'll be back to answer some questions, in any case.

But no, not that one.

Forrest ends Seventeen Dollars a Square Inch with a quadplet poem for Eric (republished in Scrapbook 177). "Quadplet," of course, is one of those invented words Forrest indulged in, so who knows what it really means, but I tried writing one for my own friend:

> *Cold, refreshing waters babble of your life,*
> *Whistling pines proffer your wisdoms to sup;*
> *In your place, the mountains rumble your name;*
> *Can I even try to shut them up?*

I'm sure I will go alone in there again in the future and appreciate its beauty anew. Forrest didn't make it back to his special place in his final hour. But when I go back some day to lie down beneath those towering pines, tilt my hat over my face to shield against the bright sun, and drift off into one more afternoon nap in that serene forest in the wilds of the Cowboy State, I know he will be resting there next to me.

I hope that place will always remain as pristine as when he first discovered it.

Two people could keep a secret. Now one of them is dead.

Drying off after a decade in the elements. The Ziploc bags were full of condensation, and these two items were together in one. "Why did I put the scissors in there?" Forrest asked me when he saw them. I didn't know, of course. I figured they belonged to King Tut or something like that. Nope. Just a pair of scissors. At some point before he secreted the chest, a simple pair of metal scissors made their way in there without him noticing. I got the sense that, even after many years of preparation, the final audacious decision to actually put the chest out there was something of a whim. I'm sure he wouldn't have liked it any other way.

Many searchers know that Seventeen Dollars a Square Inch doesn't end with just the quadplet. There were two more characters at the bottom of the page — $\Omega\Omega$. Two omegas, side by side, just like at the end of The Thrill of the Chase. I'd always thought they could possibly have been a hint to a clue in the poem, but how could they be if they were also in this earlier book about Eric Sloane? To me, there wasn't enough evidence of intent in order to consider it a hint.

E. Pairing

It's something I wanted to ask Forrest about when we met again, but I never got to. Some things will always remain a mystery, and I think that's fitting. Forrest always said he was ambivalent about whether he wanted to see the chest found in his lifetime or for the chase to last many decades after he passed, and the depth of that ambivalence profoundly revealed itself to me in the process of figuring out exactly where it was.

He was completely open with me about anything I wanted to confirm or know when we met, but his emotions were a little perplexing. I could tell there was some eagerness in finally sharing these secrets with someone, but there was also melancholy. And so perhaps it's fitting that ambivalence ends in me knowing most of the answers but him getting to keep some of them forever.

The relevance of the double omegas will go to the grave with the man who wrote the poem.

And so it is.

ΩΩ

Up until now I had been willing to accept the finder's story as far-fetched but feasible. This letter however was a bridge too far. It was littered with blatant clues to its lack of authenticity. It was clearly written with significant input from Fenn himself. Anyone familiar with Fennspeak would recognise the inconsistencies instantly.

The letter opens with the same Far T and double OO reference Fenn uses in the 'Too Far To Walk' title of his second book, an oblique hint to Stephen King and his works.

It then degenerates into a long-winded story about the finder crying after finding the treasure, then ending up laughing after realising the ridiculousness of the situation. This is a rather obvious reference to the beatitude "Blessed are those who cry for they shall laugh", which follows on from the yet to be discussed "Blessed are the meek, for they shall inherit the earth", and the defining, "Blessed are the peacemakers, for they shall be called the children of God".

The further clues within the letter are many, but the most salient is when Fenn calls the finder a "genius". This would be a truly bizarre occurrence from a man who spent over 15 years creating a cryptological masterpiece, only to have a supposed unknown from out east with little knowledge of the solution, find the target area and stumble upon the treasure. Those who have picked up on the Fennspeak aspect may have already have seen through this thinly veiled puzzle. To spell it out, if you remove the I from genius, you are left with genus, an implication that Fenn and the finder may be closer than initially thought.

The closing statement in the letter, relating to the double omegas is the perfect Segway into the next chapter. The finder's presumption that the secret of the relevance of the two omegas will go to the grave with Fenn is premature and unjustified. There is ample evidence to support the numerous interpretations of the double omega symbols. One being there are two distinct treasure hunts and as a result two endings. Then there is a more blatant, physical interpretation of the two omegas which we will get to shortly.

CHAPTER 13

SALT & PEPPER

After two years of being convinced the treasure was hidden in Colorado it had come as a massive shock that the chest had been presumably found in Wyoming. While there was suspicion about the authenticity of the finder surely the recovery of the treasure had been from the original spot. It dawned on me, for this to be the case there must be a duplicate solution to the clues within the poem. This conclusion came as another penny-drop moment.

Sprinkled within Fenn's books are photos of twins, or alternatively of his daughters, who may as well be twins they look so alike. There are also persistent references to salt and pepper. Mirror images also figure throughout the books. These aspects were all lost on me until the realisation there were possibly two solutions using the same clues, and these double images were pointers to this. Finally, Fenn provides a mega clue in his book Once Upon a While. Each chapter has a circular date stamp with the words My Two Sense emblazoned across it. Surely this is a sound-alike clue to my two scents, referring to separate trails that a sniffer dog could follow.

I had been so myopic about Ouray, I was blissfully unaware of there being a town called Winchester in Wyoming. And there it was, just downstream from Winchester, Gulch Down. Just upstream, was Thermopolis, which as the name suggests was famous for its hot springs. "Begin it where warm waters halt and take it to the canyon down". This was like shooting fish in a barrel.

The Pearl Necklace

Further up the road was Cody, a town that Fenn was very familiar with. He served on the board of directors for the Buffalo Bill Wild West Museum and spent plenty of time there over a number of years.

It looked like Fenn was up to his old tricks, starting each answer with an O, a C, or both, or a pictorial representation of a circle. With little to no effort we already had

1. Winchester - begin it where warm waters halt
2. Cody – the Home of brown

Finding 3. was a walk in the park. Just up the Shoshone River from Cody, on the way to Yellowstone is Colters Hell, which is definitely no place for the meek, in more ways than one. In the literal sense, it is a thermal area featuring fumaroles and geysers at the entrance to a narrow canyon through which rapids follow. It was first described by mountain man John Colter who was part of the Lewis and Clark expedition. It gained further prominence in 1830 when trapper Joseph Meek camped in the area with a tribe of Absarokee Indians.

3. Colters Hell -no place for the meek

I had suspected the Mummy Cave could be one of the solutions, as it is further down the road from Cody to Yellowstone and Fenn includes it in a number of his stories. This turned out to be the case.

"The end is ever drawing nigh..." The end is represented by the Omega symbol, the same shape as a cave entrance. This could also be an explanation for the double omega, as there are two caves in the overall hunt, one in the first nine clues, another in the second. In the first nine clues "Is ever" translates to "I sever". I think Fenn may have given up on folks deducing this from the poem, so tells a story in OUAW about George Dabich making him a knife from a sheep bone he found in the Mummy cave.

4. Omega Cave – the end is ever drawing nigh

It was at this point things took a bizarre turn. While flicking through "TFTW" the word Blessed caught my eye. My early years spent at Sunday School finally paid dividends. "Blessed are the meek, for they

E. Pairing

shall inherit the earth", one of the beatitudes from the New Testament sprung to mind. Further digging uncovered the English actor and author Bryan Blessed. Reading his Wikipedia profile, I knew we had struck paydirt. There were just too many coincidences for him not to be part of the solution. To name a few:

- He played Long John Silver in Treasure Island
- His first book was The Turquoise Mountain
- He wrote The Quest for the Lost World

It was then I found the mother lode,

- He had starred in Tarzan as the voice of the arch villain Clayton.

Previously I had been scouring the map to the west of Colters Hell for some likely locations fitting the O and C pattern. Clayton Mountain was a possible candidate. The Bryan Blessed confirmation inspired a flurry of activity focussed firmly on this area. Two massive discoveries immediately came to light. Firstly, I searched on-line for "Clayton Mountain Forrest Fenn Solves'. It took me straight to a Cody local who had published his solution on-line. He had also spent an extravagant amount of time searching the Clayton Mountain area for the treasure. His solution was the best I had encountered in 2 and a half years of on-line excavation. It was thoroughly researched and made compelling sense.

As well as containing numerous invaluable insights, it presented the second major discovery – the reason Fenn had chosen this area as part of the solution.

On August 21, 1937, fifteen firefighters were killed while fighting the Blackwater fires on the western slopes of Clayton Mountain. This day was Fenn's 7th birthday. At the time he and his family would have been taking the road past Clayton Mountain on the way home to Temple, Texas, from their annual holidays in Yellowstone. In an amazing twist of fate, 8 of those killed in the fire were young men from the Temple, Texas area, 1200 miles away.

The exact involvement of the Fenn family in the aftermath of the fires is unknown to the author but is likely they were impacted dearly by the return of the young men's bodies back to Texas. The events and emotion of those few days would have been indelibly burned into Fenn's psyche forever.

The forest fire was one of the deadliest in USA history. Could the reference in the poem to the blaze be related to this? Possibly, but there is another finding that underlines this area as the final resting place of Fenn's treasure. Fenn makes many references to the works of Stephen King. King wrote a book called Blaze. The central character in the book is Clayton Blaisdell, Jr - his nickname The Blaze.

With all this newly acquired knowledge onboard I emailed Cody Local. He was incredibly obliging, and we corresponded back and forth over a number of weeks. Between us we were able to thrash out a new solution using the best of his original solve and some input from myself. I was pleased with the outcome while I got the feeling he was still quite attached to his original solution.

During our correspondence he also divulged some invaluable information regarding the search area and his endeavours. Interestingly, at the time the finder had supposed spent 25 days searching the area, Cody local had been in the area looking for the treasure. He hadn't encountered anyone else at either of the carparks providing access into the area.

He enlightened me to the existence of June Creek. It entered the Shoshone River across from Mummy Cave. Of course Fenn would include June Creek in his solution, after all his dearly loved only sister was June. Cody Local assured me he had read somewhere that Fenn had said that his father never spanked his sister, offering up the answer – there'll be no paddle up your creek.

5. June Creek
6. Clayton Mountain

Studying June Creek a strong sense of déjà vu became apparent. It was Cutler Creek all over again. Fenn had found an area in Wyoming with an identical layout to the area near Ouray in Colorado. A creek enters June Creek from the left. Up that creek a delta is present, formed by two small creeks feeding the single creek. Above the delta a rocky promontory. The penultimate solutions were the same in each hunt, due to the layout being the same.

E. Pairing

7. Castle Rock & Corbenic
8. Mercedes Star

Having already solved the Colorado hunt, the final solution to the Wyoming hunt was readily apparent. Putting a circle around the Wyoming delta, it was clear the Mercedes Star was pointing back at Mummy's Cave. I grabbed a ruler and drew the line on a map of the area. Immediately something struck me. The line, with Mummy's Cave at one end and the delta at the other, was a visual representation of a bizarre story Fenn tells in TTOTC. In the story, Buffalo Cowboys, Forrest's brother Skippy sneaks up on a sleeping buffalo called Cody and ties a rope around his horns. The other end of the rope is tied to the axle of Skippy's car. In real life, Cody the buffalo, represents Cody the town. The rope represents the road toward Yellowstone, the line on the map, the axle on the car, and Mummy's Cave and the Delta the wheels on the car. If we assign the letters AXLE to the points on the line, being A for the Delta, E at Mummy Cave, the L where the line connects to the axle, and the X at a point between the Delta and the Line. Surely now it was just a matter of convincing Cody Local to venture back out into the wilderness around Clayton Mountain and collect the chest.

Snow was already falling around the Mummy Cave area when I reconnected with Cody Local. He was excited about the Axle Line theory and willing to venture out in the cold to recover the treasure. He was much less excited about the suggestion to go at night. He intimated it was scary enough in the woods around Clayton Mountain during the day let alone going in the dark. With a forecast increase in snow over the next few days Cody Local agreed to go the next day and search for the chest.

The plan was simple. Cody Local would drive his ute up highway 14 toward Mummy's Cave, turning off just before reaching it, crossing the Shoshone River over the bridge to UXU Ranch. The bridge is very similar to the one on page 6 of OUAW. The one in the book is of the Leon Bridge just outside Temple, Texas. Its inclusion in the book serves two purposes. It is a hint to Jeff Leon Bridges (and his movies) importance to the chase. It is also a pointer to the UXU bridge. He would then park his vehicle and walk to the treasure site approximately 2000 yards from the carpark, crossing June Creek and walking up the steep slope through the woods until his GPS showed he was on the Axle Line. He would then travel along the Axle Line toward the delta until he encountered the treasure chest.

Unfortunately, unlike the Colorado search with Bindi and Darion, there was no direct feed from the field to view the treasure hunt live. I would have to go to work and wait like an expectant father for the outcome. Cody Local would email me as soon as he got back home. He assured me it would be in my in-box when I got home from a hard day at the factory.

True to his word, an email boldly titled "Amazing Find" was waiting for me when I unfolded my laptop upon arriving home. I hurriedly opened the email and began reading.

"You will never believe what happened today!" it began, "I thought we found the treasure! It was exactly where you predicted it would be, wrapped in plastic, a black box exactly the same size as the treasure chest. I almost had a heart attack. Inside the box was a rusty key, but no treasure. What is going on?"

What is going on indeed?

9. Box with rusty key

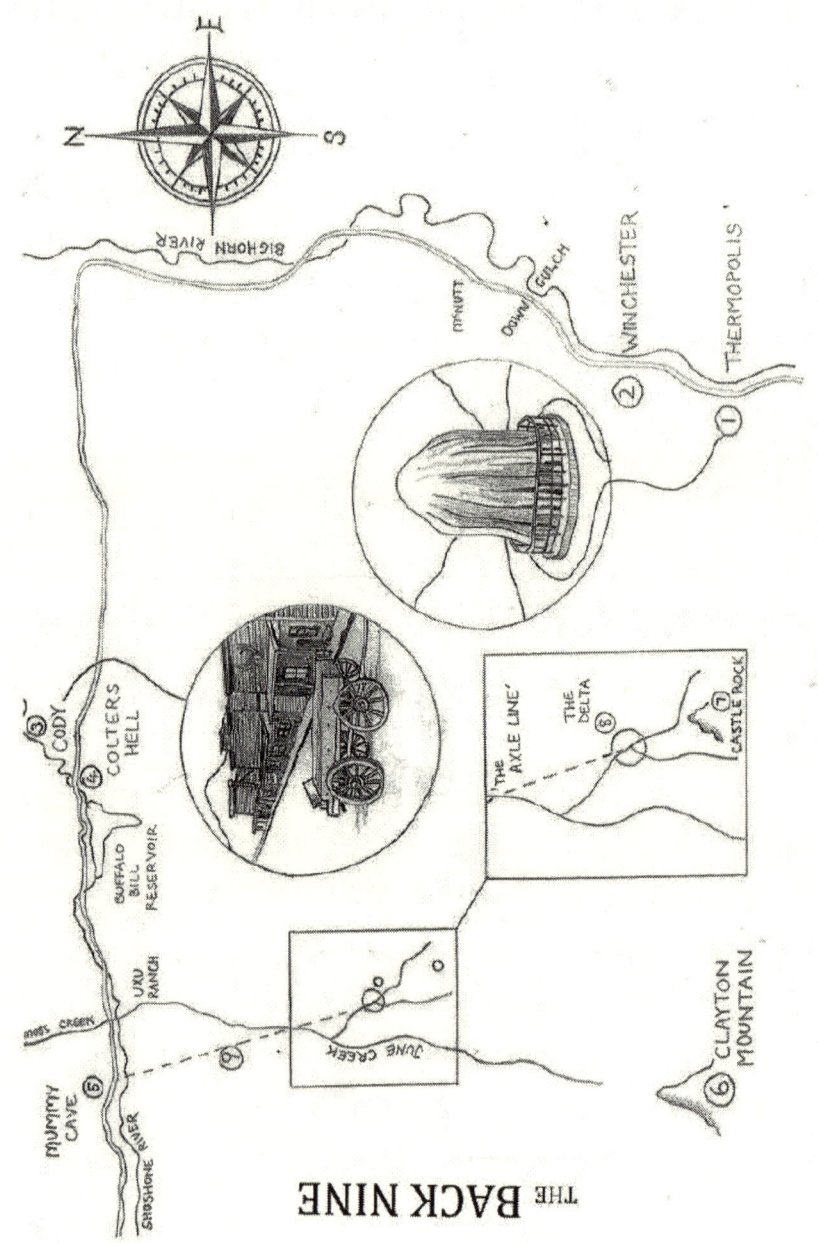

CHAPTER 14

THE BACK NINE

After the Colorado experience I was of the mind that nothing in this chase would surprise me again.

The delayed nature of the Wyoming discovery news softened the landing somewhat but still left me floored. Two complete but compatible treasure hunts, 600 miles apart, both leading to a dead end.

What was Fenn thinking? Had he really expected one person to solve both sides of this hunt, only to be left empty handed?

Over the next month Cody Local and I traded emails, discussing this and that. One evening we were going back and forth debating the merits of Cody, the town, being the home of Brown. I was of the mind Fenn was referring to the Buffalo Bill Centre of the West, buff being a shade of brown. Cody Local raised the possibility he was referring to Nancy Tia Brown, a previous Mayor of Cody. Like Fenn, she was also an art dealer and probably a friend of his. Her residence was in central Cody, not far from the museum.

Either way, I had always thought "put in" referred to entering a river. There was one small problem with this in Cody. If you "put in" to the Shoshone River below the home of Brown, you would be heading east, away from the Mummy Cave and Yellowstone.

A quick study of Cody on Google maps and a new theory quietly emerged from the laptop screen. Directly across the road from the Buffalo Bill Centre of the West lies the Cody Central Park Mini Golf attraction.

This was yet another lightbulb moment.

E. Pairing

What if, just maybe, "put in" was a corruption of "putt in".

Fenn had once said, "If I could have chosen one job in the world it would been a professional golfer. Unfortunately, my 12- handicap got in the way."

Then it dawned on me, and the flood gates opened.

Each of the treasure hunts had consisted of nine clues, each ending with a circular reference. Just like a golf course. A front nine holes, then a back nine holes.

And maybe, just maybe, the treasure was at the nineteenth hole, after all, it had always been my favourite hole on the course.

There was just one small problem, where was the nineteenth hole?

CHAPTER 15

JACKSON HOLE

All weekend hackers know the 19th hole on any golf course is the clubhouse. It is the most difficult hole to play and has wrecked many a good scorecard. But where was the clubhouse on Forrest Fenn's fictious golf course? With the front nine being just outside Ouray in Colorado, and the back nine on Clayton Mountain in Wyoming, the clubhouse could be anywhere.

Given you can usually walk from the eighteenth green to the clubhouse, and the treasure had been found in Wyoming I figured this was its most likely location. I searched on-line for Clubhouse Wyoming and listed out the top three options. Interestingly the top two were both in Jackson Hole.

The first was a children's museum called The Clubhouse. It was opened in 2011. As Fenn had published The Chase in 2010 it was unlikely, but not impossible, this was the connection we were looking for.

The second prospect on the list was an establishment called The Clubhouse at the Shooting Star Golf Club. It was the clubhouse to a magnificent golf course looking out to the Grand Teton Mountains, but it was so much more than just a golf course clubhouse. It was a luxurious western-styled resort with restaurants and bars, spas and saunas, swimming pool and firepits. It was the embodiment of many of Fenn's favourite things. If he was looking for somewhere to die, he could find a lot worse places than this.

E. Pairing

Working backwards, I figured if either of these two options were Fenn's 19th, there would have had to have been a clue at the 18th hole to lead the successful searcher to the final destination.

I emailed Cody Local. "Had there been anything unusual or special about the black box you found on the Axle line?" He replied almost immediately, "Got Covid, under the weather, can't say much but the "chest" was an old black tin with CK embossed into the lid. It was in a swallow hole in the ground, and sealed in plastic to protect it from the weather. Despite that, the key in the tin was quite rusty."

None of that seemed to point to Jackson Hole, apart from maybe the hole it was sitting in.

I racked my memory trying to recall any references Fenn had made to Jackson in his books and other writings. Nothing.

I hated to do this as I knew the consequences. I took down TTOTC, OUAW, and TFTW from the bookshelf in the war room and began to read through them for the umpteenth time. It was only a matter of time before my wife walked in and gave me her perspective.

"I thought when that guy Jack found that treasure it would be end of this business. You know it was all a hoax! Shouldn't you be out mowing the lawn, painting the house, or doing something useful?"

"Yes darling'", I responded, knowing only too well that this would provoke an even stronger response. I turned to silent mode and began reading. Unfortunately, it took until page 48 of TFTW to hit the jackpot. There it was in plain view. A story about Fenn when he was 14. He had been grounded by his father and couldn't go to the Friday Night dance with his friends. In a fortunate twist of events his father was going away for the weekend and his mother allowed him to go to the dance. He ran from his house towards the school gymnasium 1 mile away, where the dance was being held. About half way there he stopped at JACKSON Park for rest. Realising the error of his ways, he jumped up and sprinted back home to his mummy.

If you don't comprehend the relevance of this story by now you are probably reading the wrong book. In this story Fenn's mom is representative of Mummy Cave. He runs down the Axle line. Halfway along he stops at JACKSON park for rest, then turns and runs back to his Mummy. It is a defining moment in his life when he realises is true feeling for his mother.

This was good I thought, but surely if this was the ultimate clue, Fenn would have left other clues throughout his writings to the importance of Jackson. It took some digging, but they are there.

My favourite involves one of the central characters in the Colorado chase, Janice Okeson.

JAniCe oKeSON.

Discovering this brought tingles to my spine. Is this why Fenn chose Ouray and Winchester Gulch as the site for his first nine holes?

Another connection can be found in Arlington Cemetery. The realisation of the importance of the circular roads comes from the most prominent of these, directly behind the Tomb of the Unknown Soldier, JACKSON circle.

Fenn tells other stories, where, when you fact-check them, the actual reference he is making is bogus and the real location or person is JACKSON. Or he deliberately avoids referring to a place by its real name, using an alternate name instead.

This is all very interesting but at the end of the day it all pales into insignificance when the ultimate reference is understood. It delivers a bombshell that changes the whole complexion of the chase as we know it.

We all know the identity of the supposed finder, JACK Stuef. Real name Jonathon Stuef.

Was he chosen to be the finder of the treasure purely because his name matched the solution. Is the discovery of the treasure in itself just another major clue to the final resting place of the chest.

Or was the reason even deeper?

JACK SON.

Either way, a Johnny Cash song began playing in my head......

> "We got married in a fever
> Hotter than a pepper spout
> We've been talkin bout Jackson
> Ever since the fire went out
> I'm goin' to Jackson, I'm gonna mess around,
> Yeah, I'm goin' to Jackson,
> Look out Jackson town."

CHAPTER 16

WHITE XMAS IN WYOMING

With the Clubhouse at The Shooting Star Golf Resort now the nailed-on favourite to be the next stop on Forrest Fenn's magical mystery tour, we gathered the team back together to discuss the best course of action. The treasure had supposedly been found but the non-disclosure of the site left the drive to discover the truth a high priority. There was also the gnawing suspicion that the discovery letter, made public by the finder, was a coded message to those conversant in Fennspeak, and of the belief that the complete story was still there to be told.

Fenn had often intimated you needed to be on the ground at the final location to solve the closing clues to the Chase. In the War room we tossed around ideas why this would be the case.

First on the agenda was the significance of the camp oven and the rusty key Fenn had secreted at end of the Ouray and Cody hunts. It was clear that together their initials spelt CORK. But what was the importance of this?

"Perhaps it's to do with the farting references," Colt suggested, "a plug for the Home of Brown."

"Hilarious, bum boy," retorted Briar-Rose, "I think it implies a special occasion."

Silence descended on the war-room.

Suddenly Tyler leapt to his feet, "I've got it. I've got it. It is so obvious."

Colt looked up from his phone, "OK, give it to us Einstein."

"Aw, it's so obvious. I'll give you a clue. If you've been wise."

"Come on wise guy, just spill the beans," sneered Colt, starting to get a little testy.

"Okay," Tyler replied, pausing for effect. "Here it is. If you've been wise, you would find the shooting star, just like the three wise men. You know, Baby Jesus and all that stuff. It implies we need to go at Christmas."

"I think you are on to something Tyler. Christmas was a very special time for Forrest Fenn. He had arrived home from his tour of duty in Vietnam on Christmas Eve. Also Fenn always said, 'Imagination is more important than knowledge'. The three wise men were also referred to as the Magi," I lectured with gusto.

"I could never understand why there is no D in knowledge. Now I get it. It's a nod, a sign that this is a major clue."

"And of course Fenn would choose Xmas. The end to every treasure hunt is based around X."

"Either way, a white Christmas in Wyoming sounds great to me," gushed Briar-Rose enthusiastically.

"Yeah, hopefully it'll be worth the cold!"

CHAPTER 17

THE PEARL NECKLACE

The Christmas Day festivities were coming to an end. It had been a wonderful occasion with a huge lunch of turkey, ham, and all the trimmings. The sound of champagne corks exploding, and Xmas crackers popping had filled the air in the Clubhouse. Dinner was no less extravagant.

As darkness fell over Jackson Hole and the spectacular snow-covered countryside, Tyler, Colt, and I migrated outside into the chilly night air.

Most people had gone to bed including Briar-Rose, who was utterly exhausted from the travel and days events.

Like moths to a flame, the 20-odd hardy individuals still up gathered around the inferno burning furiously in the circular brick firepit beside the large swimming pool in front of The Clubhouse. Low round picnic tables strategically surrounded the fire.

Being late to the party, we found an empty table in the second row back, as the outdoor furniture closest to the inferno was already occupied.

As we settled into the comfortable leather chairs, Colt produced 3 shot glasses and a partially full bottle of Glayva from under his jacket. Unscrewing the lid off the bottle, he filled the skull-shaped glasses.

"A toast," Colt declared, pausing for effect, "to the modern-day Magi, the three wise men, who against all odds found the Shooting Star."

We downed our shots of Glayva, the raw spirit bringing instant warmth against the bitter cold.

From his jacket pocket Colt then produced the cork from the champagne bottle we had enjoyed during dinner. He rolled the cork through his fingers like a Vegas poker shark and looked at Tyler and I intently.

"Another toast," he demanded. "To the Big Boobies."

"What?" I replied incredulously. A couple of sideways glances came from those seated at the table nearest to us.

"You know, breasts, tits, melons, jugs, mammories...... Le Grand Tetons!" he cried gesturing toward the moonlit mountains in the distance.

"What? I think you've reached your limit Colt," I suggested, slightly embarrassed by my son's outburst.

"Come on you peasants," Colt whispered in a low growl, "that's what Le Grand Tetons means, Big Titties, It was named by the sex-starved early French explorers."

"Nice," smiled Tyler, "But there are 3 peaks, how does that work?"

"3's company as they say," whispered Colt under his breathe, leaning forward as if he had something secret to communicate. "What I'm going to tell you now is going to blow your minds."

He placed the cork he had been twirling through his fingers carefully on its base in front of us, and in a low monotone began to tell his story.

"To Forrest Fenn they never were three peaks. What I'm about to tell you will make your hair stand on end!"

"From a young age Fenn had a fetish. A fetish for pearl necklaces."

"No way," whispered Tyler.

"Yeah way," Colt continued, moving his chair closer to the table.

"You know that story about him running home from the school dance," Colt uttered in a barely audible tone, misty vapor coming from his mouth as he spoke.

"It was the start of a lifetime fetish."

"Motherfucker," audibly emanated from the neighbouring table.

Colt looked at Tyler and I, before easing his chair back a ways, while dragging the table gently with it, taking care not to disrupt the bottles and glasses. The cork dropped onto the floor.

As Colt recovered it, we followed suit, adjusting our chairs to reform the close circle.

Carefully placing the cork on top of the now empty Glayva bottle, Colt got back into his delivery.

E. Pairing

"The story Fenn tells in OUAW about Hiccups on the golf course is a pretty straight forward word puzzle, describing the scene behind you. Hi C cups."

Colt looked down at the cork, then looked directly into each of our faces to be sure we were keeping up. He continued.

"You know the false treasure at the end of the two hunts, the Camp Oven, and the Rusty Key."

"How could we forget," I whispered encouragingly.

"CORK was the simple answer, the real answer was COCK!

Camp Oven Chest Key.

Chest Key is the solution needed to unlock the final chapter to the chase. Brilliant, as it is actually a CHEST key that is required."

Looking back down at the cork on the Glayva bottle, it formed the perfect phallic statement.

"When Fenn looks at the Grand Tetons he doesn't see three breasts. He sees two C cups with an oversized cock between them. Look quickly down, your quest two Cs! Just take the chest, and go in peace!"

"The last thing Fenn placed in the treasure chest before he closed the lid was a fetish necklace with 39 amulets on it. He always said the last thing he placed in the chest was especially important to solving the hunt. Everyone focussed on the 39 amulets, one a golden jaguar, a possible clue to the Jackson jaguars, and even more likely, a probable link to the book 'The 39 Steps'. All important, but the critical clue was the word fetish."

My mind was now working overtime. This was a lot to take in. Was Fenn's fixation with inter-mammory stimulation a strategy to remain faithful to his wife but still make use of his abundant charm and generous endowment?

Colt produced a bottle of port from nowhere and filled his glass. There was no toast this time. He took a quick sip from the shot glass, checked we were listening intently, and continued.

"You know the story about Jackie K, and the clear implication Fenn had intimate relations with her. Look closely at the photo of her sitting at the typewriter. She is wearing a double-strain pearl necklace. She thanked him then and thanked him again in the morning."

Colt drained his glass and refilled it. This time he paused as if realising his previous oversight, reaching out to fill the other two glasses on the table.

"There is another vital clue in that story. Strong is The Men in Black theme", he went on, sounding remarkably like Yoda."

"I think he used Jackie K in this fanciful story for two reasons. First for her initials JK. Throughout the chase Fenn uses consecutive letters from the alphabet, but that's a story for another day. In this case JK is a hint at Agent J and Agent K from Men in Black. Look at how many photos there are throughout his books of Fenn in his dark sunnies."

Yeah, and often in the company of actress Chrissie Snow I thought to myself. I sipped my port and it suddenly dawned on me the relevance of that connection as we sat here surrounded by the Christmas Snowfall.

"If you are Men in Black fans like me you will remember, the treasure at the end of that movie was supposedly hidden on Orion's belt in a remote galaxy."

"Gentlemen," Colt announced, raising his voice slightly, "if you look to the heavens above Le Grand Tetons, you will see the constellation Orion - The Hunter."

"And those three bright stars in a row are Orion's belt."

"No way," said Tyler incredulously.

"Yeah way," Colt echoed back.

"But that's not the half of it. Orion's Belt is also known as the String of Pearls!"

"No fucking way," exclaimed Tyler louder than he intended. "Sitting right there above Fenn's Nob."

"Maybe they will rename it that one day, or perhaps a more acceptable Fenn's Peak?"

A collective grin came to our faces, as if we were now in possession of some exclusive secret.

"There's still more," Colt continued. "See those stars below Orion's Belt. They are the hunter's sword, hanging down between his legs."

"You said there were two reasons that Fenn used JK in his story."

"Yeah, the other is obscure but I'm sure it's right."

"We all know JK was the first lady. Fenn drops a major clue in Chapter 13 of TFTW. In bold red lettering he puts the word 'First'. Then on the opposite page, he writes 'first' but leaves out the letter l. I always figured this was Fenn emphasizing his rule "leave me and I out of it". However, it is in fact a rather clever word puzzle. It's not an 'I' that is missing but a lower-case L. The answer to the puzzle is 'First no L', get it, First Noel."

E. Pairing

Tyler and I stared at Colt in total disbelief.

"You do know what First Noel is, don't you," Colt queried.

"Yeah of course. I'm just blown away by your genius," I replied, wiping a small tear from my eye.

"It's so chilly out here, it's making my eyes water," I whispered, trying to hide my fatherly pride.

"Me too," Colt replied, tapping his phone that was sitting on the table. It burst to life and his carefully choreographed show went to a new level, as music gently emerged from its speaker....

> The first Noel, the angels say
> To Bethlehem's shepherds as they lay.
> At midnight watch, when keeping sheep,
> The winter wild, the light snow deep.
>
> *Noel, Noel, Noel, Noel*
> *Born is the King of Israel.*
>
> The shepherds rose, and saw a star
> Bright in the East, beyond them far,
> Its beauty gave them great delight,
> This star it set now day nor night.
>
> *Noel, Noel, Noel, Noel*
> *Born is the King of Israel.*
>
> Now by the light of this bright star
> Three wise men came from country far;
> They sought a king, such their intent,
> The star their guide where'er it went.
>
> *Noel, Noel, Noel, Noel*
> *Born is the King of Israel.*
>
> Then **drawing nigh** to the northwest,
> O'er Bethlehem town it took its rest;
> The wise men learnt its cause of stay,
> And found the place where Jesus lay.

Noel, Noel, Noel, Noel
Born is the King of Israel.

"Beautiful, Colt, truly beautiful," I praised.

"But how does it take us to the treasure?" queried Tyler, bringing me back down to earth.

"I'm thinking we really are at the pointy end. Here's how I see it," I responded.

"The 39 Steps. We did 18 holes around Ouray and Cody, and now we are at the Clubhouse, the 19th. Two 19's is 38, plus one is 39. We had to come here now, at Xmas to get the location when the constellation is directly above Le Grand Tetons, then we need to come back and retrieve the treasure in summer. 2 x 19 + 1 trip to get the treasure. Simple but perfect math."

"So what's so special about now?" queried Tyler again.

"Everything is fixed, apart from the Hunter. Each night it moves to a slightly different position in the sky". I theorised, thinking out loud. "Draw a line through his sword down to a point on earth. But to where?"

Silence fell upon the three wise men. It must have been 10 minutes we sat sipping our port and contemplating the hunter, his sword, the heavens above, and the earth below.

"I think I got it," whispered Tyler.

''When we completed the 18 holes, we looked for the Clubhouse."

''We also had a rusty key that gave us CORK, but that turned out to also be COCK."

"I think it's a word continuation puzzle, the answer to which is COCK PIT. After all, Fenn was a fighter pilot. He felt alive in his cockpit, with his joystick in his hand."

"So where's the location," queried Colt.

"The fire pit, it's right under our noses. It's the ring of fire. You know, Johnny Cash – the man in black," shot back Tyler.

"Yes," I concurred. "Remember the stone circle at The Flamingo. I get it now, The Flaming O."

"You draw a line from the hunter's sword, representing a man's penis, to the firepit, representing a woman's counterpart. The treasure is somewhere along the line, but there's one small problem. The line is different against the background landscape depending on where you are

E. Pairing

standing. There must be a fixed spot to carry out this task," I speculated, making it up as I went along.

"Jesus," exclaimed Tyler, "I thought Fenn said a child could figure this out."

We looked at each other and then the bottle of port.

"Enough hunting for one night," I suggested.

Both Colt and Tyler nodded. "Let's just enjoy one last drink and sleep on this final conundrum."

"A final toast," cried Colt. "To the cockpit," as he raised his glass to the still roaring fire.

"To the cockpit," Tyler and I responded.

"To the cockpit," the gang at the next table cheered, raising their beer glasses to the heavens.

Weighed down by the food and drink, we made our way back to our rooms.

Once in bed, sleep came easy.

CHAPTER 18

BREAKFAST IN AMERICA

I woke from a deep sleep as sun poured through the uncurtained window. The view across the snow-covered golf course to the Grand Tetons was breath-taking. In the foreground the firepit was still smouldering away, and staff in black aprons and hats were clearing the debris from the surrounding tables.

Reluctantly I texted Briar-Rose to see what time they were heading down to breakfast.

"In about an hour," she texted back.

I was glad. I lay back, closed my eyes, and pondered what was surely the final hurdle in the chase. Where would Fenn have been when he drew the line connecting the hunter's sword to the fire pit? Unfortunately, I was finding it difficult to think, as every time I thought of firepit the Johnny Cash song "Ring of Fire" would come into my head and refuse to leave.

> "I fell in to a burning ring of fire
> I went down, down, down, and the flames went higher
> And it burns, burns, burns,
> the ring of fire
> the ring of fire"

Frustrated I opened my eyes and gazed back out the window. It was in that moment it came to me.

E. Pairing

Fenn would have been lying on one of the beds in this wonderful establishment when he came up with his grand finale. The huge bedroom windows affording the magnificent views out to the snow-capped mountains were like large paintings. Drawing a line from the stars in the sky back down to the firepit by the pool would be easily accomplished, then a point on that line readily established as marking the final resting place of the treasure chest on the mountain range in the distance. He could mark the window frame on either side to indicate the second line. There was only one small problem. Which room had Forrest chosen as the keeper of his closely guarded secret?

Excited as a dog with two tails, I leapt out of bed and quickly showered. I couldn't wait to get down to breakfast to fill the team in on the latest theory.

Down at breakfast we found a table away from the other guests, by a window looking out to the mountains. Tyler had briefed Briar-Rose on the discussions of the previous night. She was somewhat taken aback by the content of the solution but agreed the evidence was compelling.

As we ate from the selection of Danish pastries and fresh fruit, Briar-Rose held us to account. "You guys really don't think Fenn would actually have performed those acts on his mother and Jackie Kennedy do you?"

"Of course not," I replied immediately, while Tyler and Colt both shook their heads in agreement.

"Good," she retorted. "Those stories are analogies. Haven't you peasants ever heard of Oedipus?"

"I've heard of Eatalottapuss," Colt joked. "She was a lesbian dinosaur."

Briar-Rose narrowed her eyes and glared at Colt. "Oedipus, from Greek mythology. You must have heard of the Oedipus Complex, where a son kills his father due to his affection for his mother."

"Motherfucker," Colt mumbled under his breath.

"In the Greek myth it happened unwittingly without Oedipus being aware of it. Here, read the story on-line, she said, passing Colt her phone."

Colt took the phone and began reading quietly aloud,

"The Oedipus Complex is derived from Sophocles' *Oedipus Tyrannus*. In the story, Oedipus learned that he was cursed to kill his father and sleep with his mother.

Here is the history of the prophecy that doomed Oedipus

- Laius, who ruled Thebes at the time, was told the prophecy that his son would kill him and sleep with his wife.
- To ensure the prophesy wouldn't come true, he and his wife gave their baby son to one of their slaves, who was to take the baby to Mt. Cithaeron, which was haunted by wild beasts.

However, the slave felt pity for the baby, so he gave him to another shepherd from the city of Corinth located on the other side of the mountain.

King Polybus of Corinth was presented with the baby and decided to bring him up himself.

When Oedipus was older, someone calls him a bastard.

He decided to leave Corinth for Delphi, so he could learn of his parentage at the oracle of Apollo in Delphi.

There he was given the news that he would kill his father and sleep with his mother.

To prevent the oracle from coming true, Oedipus left Corinth and headed to Thebes.

On the way he ran into an old man driving a wagon at a place where three roads cross. The man ordered Oedipus to move off the road, but he refused.

He became aggressive and killed the man and what he thought to be all the guards.

Before Oedipus could enter Thebes, he had to solve the riddle the Sphinx, who guarded the entrance to the city, asked him. No one had ever solved the riddle before and as a consequence, they were killed by the Sphinx.

The riddle was, "Which animal has one voice, but two legs in the morning, three in the afternoon, and four legs at dusk, being slowest on three?" Oedipus answered correctly with the answer, "Man."

The city welcomed Oedipus and offered him the vacant job of king and the marriage to Laius' widow, Jocasta.

Years passed while Oedipus was king of Thebes. He had four children by Jocasta.

E. Pairing

Eventually the city was infected by a plague. Oedipus promised to save his city, so he ordered his brother-in-law Creon to consult the oracle at Delphi.

He returned with news that the plague was caused by the unpunished murderer who killed Laius. Oedipus cursed the killer, but Tiresias said that Oedipus was the killer.

Oedipus was furious and blamed Tiresias and Creon for creating such a story to dethrone him so that they could have power.

Jocasta explained to Oedipus that robbers killed Laius at a place where three roads crossed. Oedipus remembered that he killed a man at such a place.

He contemplated the possibility of himself being the killer, but Jocasta reassured him that a witness saw several robbers kill Laius.

Oedipus sent for the witness, so the issue could be resolved.

While he waited, a Corinthian messenger arrived with news that Polybus had died, so Oedipus would be King of Corinth.

Oedipus told the messenger that he could not go back while his mother was alive.

Surprise overwhelmed Oedipus, for the messenger told him that she was not his mother. He explained that he was given the baby many years ago by a Theban shepherd.

Jocasta then realized that Oedipus was her son.

The witness finally arrived and revealed that he was given the baby by Jocasta and passed it to the messenger because he did not want to kill him.

Oedipus realizes the truth and goes to tell Jocasta, but she had already killed herself.

He blinds himself and was ordered to leave Thebes by Creon, the new king.

"My god, that's a cheerful story," Colt murmured, "Its sorta put me off my croissant."

We all sat and stared down at our plates.

Colt continued to scroll through stuff on Briar-Rose's phone.

"Hey, look at this," he blurted out, suddenly rejuvenated by what he had found.

"It says here that the song 'The End' by the Doors, is about the Oedipus Complex."

"Man, I loved that song at the beginning of Apocalpyse Now," I reminisced.

> This is the end, beautiful friend
> This is the end, my only friend,
> The end of our elaborate plans
> The end of everything that stands

"As a Vietnam vet Fenn would have known that movie intimately," I offered up, "But what is the significance of all this?"

"I think it's the riddle," suggested Briar-Rose. "Fenn was the ultimate Riddler - an adversary to another Man in Black - Batman. Also there's the search for the holy grail, the Fisher King, and the need to answer the final riddle. The riddle in the Oedipus myth is right up Fenn's alley.

What walks on four legs in the morning, two in the afternoon, and three at night?

"Yeah, that would have intrigued Fenn as he felt he had three legs most of his life," joked Colt, once again causing his sister to shake her head in disbelief.

CHAPTER 19

THE RIDDLE

In the mid-2010's discussion began on-line that the poem contained a riddle that was crucial to solving the Chase. As no one seemed to know what the riddle was, but were aware of its existence, suspicion immediately arose that this was a Fenn leak. It had been suspected for some time, Fenn frequented on-line sites under bogus pseudonyms, inserting comments and clues to influence the direction of the hordes searching for the treasure. The existence of a riddle would be in keeping with the Fisher King theme, and the historical requirement for knights venturing to Corbenic to ask, or answer, a question to release the King from his predicament. Within his books Fenn also hints at the existence of a riddle. Many of his stories are merely extensions of popular everyday riddles, such as 'Why did the chicken cross the road?', spun out into a humdrum story in TTOTC.

Analysing the poem to unearth a riddle proved difficult. Every line in the verse was open to question. Where was there? What is it? Why is the treasure bold?

A clue to the riddles existence and its composition was uncovered in detailed analysis of the first verse. The anagram at the end of the second line is derived from TREASURE BOLD, the most likely solution being DOUBLE ARREST. The answer to the third line is derived from the anagram SECRET WHERE giving TWREE CHEERS, and the anagrammatic answer to the fourth line is FOR CHIPETA AND WISE OLD NDN.

The Pearl Necklace

Following the trend of DOUBLE, THREE, FOR, the answer to the first line would be singular, and possibly in response to a riddle asked within the line. Re-arranging the first 15 letters of the line, especially the GONE ALON(E) component, and we have AS I HAVE A LONG ONE, posing the riddle 'What is a long one to a dying man'?

As an aside, 'AS I' references the American novel As I Lay Dying. It is extremely apt, given Fenn's personal circumstance while writing the chase. The storyline in the book also sets the overall scene to the theme of the chase, and the journey of a body to its final resting place.

On discovering the riddle in the poem, I was immediately convinced the answer was A REST. A dying man is definitely in for a long rest, and the answer fitted perfectly with the answers to the following three lines of the poem,

A REST
DOUBLE ARREST
TWREE CHEERS
FOR CHIPETA AND WISE OLD NDN

Subsequent events and new discoveries threw up alternate answers to the riddle. BELT became the next possible solution. Was it possible Fenn was posing a riddle with multiple correct answers?

BELT works well as the probable solution as it is the first two and last two letters of the fifth line of the poem. Fenn's turquoise buckled belt was one of his prized possessions, and the belt concept matches the hole-to-hole layout of the treasure hunt.

Clearly RIDE HOME was another possible starter as Fenn refers to the long ride home throughout the chase.

However, the deeper I descended into the Chase the more I became convinced "As I have a long one" isn't so much a riddle, as a statement. In his letter the finder confides Fenn was a man comfortable with his masculinity. This seems a strange thing to say, and stands out in the letter like the proverbial.

Given the letter was most likely written with input from Fenn, is it a blatant pointer to this unlikely aspect to the story. The discovery of this facet of the chase puts an uncomfortable shadow across the whole enterprise. Once aware of this aspect it is difficult not to read his books, and the poem, without the new perspective tarnishing the stories and

E. Pairing

giving a darker, more sordid outlook. It appears Fenn's most prized possession was his own joystick. Take a look back through his books and each photo with this in mind. In addition to this, in his books Fenn tells a number of stories involving roosters. It was always assumed these were a reference to Rooster Coogan in True Grit. Maybe they were, but it now appears they were also a clue to a larger, more base element to the chase.

More disturbingly, the final "treasure" at the end of each leg of the chase provides a vital clue to the answer to the riddle. The item found at the end of the Ouray hunt was a rusty old camp oven. The item at the end of the Wyoming hunt was a rusty old key to the chest.

It appears these two treasures provide the answer to the riddle, "As I have a long one"

Camp Oven, Chest Key

Fenn also said he could have been a professional golfer if not for his twelve handicap. It highly probable Fenn was hinting his handicap was measured in inches.

Another prominent theme throughout the Chase is "The Last Stand". It is mentioned in many of Fenn's stories. Taking the stand in court, the diving stand, Custer references. I never really understood the significance of this theme. I had theorised the treasure was maybe hidden near an old hunting stand in the forest, and finding the stand was key to finding the treasure.

Whenever I wanted to get a perspective of anything Fenn I would go and talk to my father. They were of the same era, born only two years apart. They had similar backgrounds and upbringing. They both became collectors of things and lovers of literature. They both had served in the military and had an abundance of stories to tell about their pasts.

One afternoon my father and I were sitting in his lounge. For no particular reason we were discussing great battles in history. We touched on Waterloo, Culloden, and Hastings. Eventually we got around to the battle of Little Big Horn and Custers Last Stand. Out of the blue he said, "What is six inches long with an arrow through it?". I immediately got the joke but had never heard of the male erection referred to as the stand before. It immediately completed another connection between one of Fenn's key themes and Fenn's greatest treasure.

The concluding piece of evidence hinting at Fenn's oversize appendage is the use of the Mercedes symbol and the peace symbol. In the solution at the end of each of the nine holes Fenn uses the stickman

The Pearl Necklace

with the turquoise belt overlaid on the Mercedes sign at the delta. If you overlay the peace sign on this it gives the turquoise man his final feature. Given the story of the Fisher King and his wounded penis, this is all the more appropriate.

I filled the group in on the bedroom window theory. Amazingly Colt had independently come up with a similar suggestion albeit by slightly different means. He began regaling us with a story of him undressing for bed then lying naked looking out at the moonlit Tetons. It was there we stopped him and left the rest to our already damaged imagination.

As we ate from the selection of Danish pastries and fresh fruit, I put the million-dollar question to the team. Which room in the Clubhouse would Fenn have used when creating his ultimate final solution?

It was suggested we ask at reception if we could go back through their records to check if Fenn had stayed there in Christmas 2009. We ruled this out as we figured he would have almost certainly used a different name. We also didn't want to draw any undue attention to ourselves.

"Surely Fenn must have given a clue to the Room Number somewhere in one of his stories, or maybe even the poem," suggested Briar-Rose.

"What about that story about the Dude Motel?", chimed in Tyler, "Fenn said they always stayed in Room 4,"

Yeah," agreed Tyler. "Didn't it involve a weird story about Ronald Reagan climbing through a back window into a motel unit."

By now Colt was scrolling through his phone checking out Ronald Reagan.

"It says here on Reagans Wiki bio his father's name was Jack. That makes him Jack son. And surely that makes the small window he climbed through Jack son hole."

"Bingo" I cried.

"Bingo indeed" added Colt, "Though never did get that story about Fenn playing bingo one rainy night in Eunice, Louisiana."

"Bingo," cried Briar-Rose, "I get it. Bing Crosby, I'm dreaming of a white Christmas."

"How does it work though?", questioned Colt, "if you only had the poem, how could you possibly find Room 4?"

Once again silence fell over the team.

"How about this. We know you get an A for effort. Maybe the room is A4," suggested Tyler.

"Brilliant," I cried. "Is there a Room A4 here at the Clubhouse?"

E. Pairing

"Let's find out," Colt volunteered, pulling out his phone. "Can I order a bottle of Bollinger champagne to Room A4 please."

"Certainly Mr. Prescott," came the reply, "I will ring back on your room phone to confirm the order."

Finishing the call, Colt snapped his phone shut and announced triumphantly, "Mr. Prescott is in for a surprise."

"Very good Colt, but we now have another problem. How are we going to get into Room A4?"

CHAPTER 20

FORAY INTO DARKNESS

Over the back end of breakfast we had come up with a number of devious plans to get the Prescott's to vacate Room 4A to allow us access to solve the final clue. However, most of them involved slightly unethical and underhanded activities that we had vowed not to entertain in our quest to secure the treasure.

Colt had suggested we have a message delivered to their room advising them of a death in the family for which they would have to leave immediately. This was voted down as being too high a risk and too easily uncovered as being untrue prior to their departure. Tyler's idea was to break into the room while they were out skiing and flood the room by leaving a tap on. This scheme certainly had merit but was considered impractical due to the illegality and the cost of the damage incurred. Briar-Rose's contribution was along similar lines. In our school days back in Australia we would get the seeds off the black wattle tree, crush them, then spit on them to create an horrendous stench that would cause any room to be vacated. Like Tyler's idea, this was also considered dangerous and too risky, and where were we going to find black wattle seeds in Wyoming any way.

After much discussion we decided to go with a much more conventional plan. We figured the Prescott's would be spending most of the days out in the countryside, skiing or hiking in the snow. At night they would be eating and socialising in the Shooting Star's restaurants and bars. During this time we would be able to pick the lock to their room and carry out the reconnaissance required. So our plan was simple.

E. Pairing

Today would be spent observing the Prescott's to establish the make-up to their family, their typical movements, their social preferences, and even getting close enough to converse with them regarding their future plans. There was only one small problem as we finished off our breakfast. We had no idea who the Prescott's were.

Being short on options, we estimated they would have also just finished breakfast and be looking to head out for the day. Skulking around in the corridor outside Room 4A was chosen as the best course of action. Briar-Rose, being the least conspicuous of our group was despatched to the upstairs hallway. Dressed in black to resemble one of the house staff it didn't take long for success. Only minutes after arriving, a group emerged from the room, dressed for day on the slopes. Four in all, the Prescott's consisted of mum and dad in their 50's, and a teenage son and daughter. Mr. Prescott senior was tall, slender, and balding, his wife an attractive blonde. The children were the all-American teenage pair, good-looking, blonde, and sporty. Briar-Rose couldn't resist engaging them in conversation.

"Morning folks, would you like me to make-up your room while you're out," BR announced keenly.

"Sure, we're going up Casper for the day, should be back around 6."

"Awesome," responded Briar-Rose. "Just leave the door open, I'll get on to it now. You folks have a wonderful day up on the slopes."

Hardly believing her luck, she texted Tyler, as the Prescott's disappeared down the stairs at the end of the corridor.

Within minutes we were congregated in Room 4A looking out the huge window in the main bedroom. It was just as we had imagined, like a large painting of the Grand Tetons. On page 50 of 'Once Upon A While' there is a picture of a person who looks suspiciously like Fenn putting a spot on a painting of a mountain range. This was our challenge now, to calculate a spot on the window, where, when viewed from the correct spot in the room would reveal the position of the treasure in the Grand Tetons.

We were sure the position of the chest was determined by creating two lines across the window that would form an X marking the treasures resting place. The trajectory of the first line had already been established. Connecting the fire-pit to the stars representing the sword of the hunter constellation in the sky above the Tetons proved to be an exercise in guesswork. The firepit was tucked in behind the swimming pool in the foreground out the window. Using the umbrellas on the tables around the pit it was relatively easy to establish the site of the fire hole. Estimating the position of the hunter's sword was a little more problematic. We had seen it clear in the sky at midnight the last two nights so were confident of its approximate place above Fenn's Peak.

Taking a small hammer from the leather tool bag we had brought along in preparation for this exercise, I tacked a tiny nail into the top of the wooden window surround. Another tack was then added into the bottom of the window surround below the fire-pit. A ball of black string was now needed to complete the task. Placing a loop over the top nail the string was pulled down tightly across the window and tied off to the bottom nail. Perfect, half the job finished.

The second line to create the X on the window was based on a number of theories that were yet to be proven. The ideas were derived from multiple aspects within Fenn's books.

The first was centred on a picture on page 188 of 'too far to walk'. It was of an artist gesturing in front of a large easel. On the easel are four X's. If a cross was drawn connecting the 4 X's it would identify an exact spot on the painting.

The second theory was based around the ant theory from the end of the Ouray hunt. Figuring it would feature in the hunt sometime in the future we had secured an UV torch during one of our many visits to Walmart.

Pulling the curtains and closing the doors to the room, it fell into darkness. Switching on the UV torch immediately reveal anything. However lying on the floor to examine the bottom edge of the window surround it became apparent there were two UV reflective beads imbedded into the wood. Taking a chair from the table and standing atop it, it confirmed the presence of two further beads on the top surface of the window trim.

This was a masterstroke by Fenn. If someone was to find the beads by chance, and somehow link them to the chase, they would think they formed an X upon the window, giving a false position as to the site of the treasure. However we were one step ahead, having deciphered a number of stories in Fenn's memoirs pertaining motel rooms and bedrooms, that gave the true perspective on the reflective beads.

The first tale was a continuation of the story regarding Ronald Reagan climbing through the small back window into the motel room

E. Pairing

at the Dude. This story has already been highlighted as a clue to Jackson Hole. It also hides another significant clue.

A little-known fact about the Republican president was he was originally a Democrat, the party represented by the donkey. Fenn always felt he was a donkey in the bedroom himself. In a truly bizarre story in 'too far to walk' Fenn tells a tale about his two aptly named donkeys Buttercup and Lollipop. He intimates in the story that if you allowed Buttercup to suck your finger she would follow you anywhere, even to the upstairs bedroom. Looking past the perverted thoughts that immediately come to mind, we figured this work of fiction serves two purposes.

Firstly, it dictates the position you need to take in the room to establish the correct site of the treasure established by the cross on the window, that position being where the donkey was standing at the end of the main bed. Secondly it dictates the letter formed by the four reflective beads is not indeed an X but in fact a Z. To arrive at this solution took an acute awareness of Fenn's appreciation of the English alphabet, and extension of his obsession with the Men in Black theme.

Due to his love of letters we had always suspected Fenn would use Z as the climactic end to the chase, and the mark of Zorro would be the definitive blaze.

In this instance he has a donkey, Buttercup, representing Ronald Reagan (RR) positioned between the Grand Tetons (OO), and the UV beads forming a giant Z across the landscape window, spelling out Zorro. Motherfucker. I thought this was going to be child's play.

Working quickly we tacked a couple more nails into the window surround, and strung the string between the nails to form the long axis of the letter Z. It made for a very narrow X.

Fenn was a very precise man, who loved aesthetically pleasing things. This just didn't feel right. We calculated maybe the Z was to be viewed from outside of the building, by the firepit, with the Z the other way around. Colt took a quick photo from the designated spot before re-stringing the Z from the other direction. He was coming to the end of the task when the sound of a key in the door made us stop in our tracks. "Fuck," mumbled Colt, as our hearts jumped into our mouths.

Briar-Rose shot out into the lounge area to meet whoever was opening the door. Colt, Tyler, and I scrambled to get the tools and string back into the tool bag, after taking a quick snap of the X from the designated spot at the end of the bed.

"Mr. Prescott, you're back earlier than expected. How was your skiing?"

"What are you still doing in here?" demanded a clearly agitated Mr. Prescott, "How long does it take to service a room."

"Apologies, Mr. Prescott, but I found an issue with your air conditioning and had to call in a service crew. They are just finishing the job in the main bedroom."

"Ok, is it fixed?" he demanded abruptly.

"I think so. They are just packing up their tools now," Briar-Rose responded looking through the door into the bedroom. "We will get out of your way."

"That would be much appreciated," Prescott answered in a more pleasant tone. "It hasn't been the morning we had planned."

With that, we hurriedly left Room 4A, shuffling past the rest of the Prescott family in the hallway.

Realising it was only a matter of time before our cover was blown, we ran to our room and hurriedly packed our belongings into our packs. Crossing the courtyard to the resort carpark, we could see Prescott about 50 yards away, talking to one of the staff outside reception. He was pointing in our direction and began walking towards us, gesturing to the staff member to follow.

Fumbling with the keys to the Wrangler I managed to unlock the vehicle. By now Prescott was running across the carpark. Throwing my pack into the back seat I jumped into the driver's seat and pressed the ignition. As the vehicle burst into life, I dropped the clutch, crashing over the curbing, through the garden ahead, and onto the exit driveway.

"Hold on," screamed Tyler, "Colt's not on board."

I hit the brakes as Colt emerged from the garden, eluding a despairing dive from Prescott.

He leapt onto the running-board, and we sped out of the resort with the back passenger door still flailing open and Colt holding on for dear life.

CHAPTER 21

THE LAST SUPPER

Our unplanned exodus from the Shooting Star necessitated an abrupt change of plan. We now needed to find accommodation where we could lie low and not draw attention to ourselves for a couple of days until our flight out of Jackson.

With the exact spot where the treasure had been hidden safely known, we now just had to stay out of trouble and wait it out until Spring. It was the end of a 4-year odyssey to find the spot, but that seemed to have limited relevance at this point in time.

Driving into town we checked online for the available motel options.

"What about this one?", suggested BR, showing her phone to Colt and Tyler.

"Amazing but too much like the Shooting Star. We need something down and dirty where we can hole up and hide away."

"What about this then," BR continued, "The Antler Inn, on West Pearl Ave."

"Looks perfect, right in town, perfect. Do they have a room with a spa?" replied Tyler.

"We're about to find out," I responded, turning off the Teton Pass Highway onto the road into Jackosn Hole village.

Ten minutes later we were unpacking the ute and lugging our bags up to our second storey room. Once settled in, I looked at the team, strewn across the two couches in the motel room. The events of the last few hours that taken their toll, and group were looking spent. In an effort to lift their spirits, I put an idea to them I had been thinking about since our discoveries at the Shooting Star.

"We've spent the last 4 years in search for this treasure. We've had some wild experiences, almost died a couple of times in the process. We might not have found the treasure, but we've had some great adventures. Let's make our last night one to remember. How about tomorrow night we put the chase to bed in style. We'll have a lavish feast in our room reliving our favourite stories."

"Better still, to make it more real, how about we dress up as our favourite Fenn character and re-enact their relevance to the Chase," suggested BR.

"If we're going to do this, I'm gunna be Zorro," jumped in Tyler without giving it a second thought.

"Well if you're going to be Zorro, I'm gunna be Doc Holliday," Colt echoed backed enthusiastically, using his fingers as pistols.

"You're going to have to wait to see who I am going to be," BR said enchantingly.

I was rapt in the response to my suggestion and suddenly became uncharacteristically gushy.

"You know, the real treasure in this whole crazy adventure has been you guys. We may not have found the chest, but it has been worth every cent and every minute we have spent on it."

"Yeah, yeah," responded Colt, clearly uncomfortable with the new found emotion, "We all know you'll be coming as Forrest Fenn."

Next day we were late rising. We headed out into the freezing cold to find breakfast at one of the local cafes. The town was blanketed in snow, which made for a beautiful but uncomfortable existence. We walked down Cache St, past the famed elk antler arches in the Town Square, to The Bunnery. Once inside, we enjoyed the warmth, and the delicious array of pancakes and other baked goodies. Being still nervous about the events of the previous day, we spent most of the time sheltering behind the available newspapers to hide our presence to the other patrons.

On completing breakfast, we headed across the road to the Browse and Buy second-hand store at the local church. It turned out to be an absolute gold mine, ideal for finding items for our costumes that night. Colt disappeared into the menswear section where he managed to uncover a pair of black cowboy boots with fancy stitching that fitted him perfectly. He also was able to score a black Stetson, belt, and waistcoat

E. Pairing

that made for an authentic Doc Holliday minus the essential side arms needed to complete the costume.

Tyler found the going a bit tougher but did find some black jeans and a matching black shirt. Likewise, Briar-Rose found a well-worn old coat and a silky white dress that had us scratching our heads as to her chosen character, though we suspected Snow White and the wicked witch.

Next stop was the Jackson Hole Toy Store, that just happened to be in the next street. It too was a veritable treasure trove, an Aladdin's cave of cherished pastimes and childhood memories. It didn't take us long to collect the items needed to complete our costumes, a golden bow and arrow, six-shooter cap guns, a zorro mask, a black cape, and a sombrero cordobes to match.

Laden with our purchases, we made our way back through the snow, via the bottle shop, to the Antler Inn. Relieved to have survived the mission without incident, we settled down to a relaxing afternoon, spent organising our costumes and refining our acts for the night ahead.

CHAPTER 22

THE CHILL OF THE THRACE

BR returned from the bedroom wearing only a short white dress with a gold braided cord tied around the waist. On her head was a wreath made from an old holly decoration, the kind you would see hanging on people's front doors at Christmas. In her right hand was a toy bow and arrow of gold, and in her left hand, an assortment of other items that couldn't be made out in the darkened motel room.

Sitting down in the throne-like chair beside the circular dining table, she reached out and put one of the mystery items in the middle of table. It was a short, fat candle over which she placed a small, rusty tripod. Upon the tripod she positioned a shallow, glass dish containing what looked to be a mixture of dried herbs.

With a flick of her fingers she created fire, igniting the candle below the dish. Immediately the herbs began to give off a sweet aroma, much like incense but with a hint of Coloradan green. It had a heady effect, bringing peace and warmth to the gathering.

After several minutes silence, BR began to speak.

"Good evenings my friends," she announced theatrically. "I am Artemis, daughter of Zeus, twin sister of Apollo, and goddess of the hunt."

"The story I am about to tell you is based in the sacred Greek town of Delphi. My father Zeus determined the site of Delphi when he sought to find the centre of Gaia, his Grandmother Earth. He sent two eagles flying from the eastern and western extremities and the path of the eagles crossed over Delphi where the navel of Gaia was found. The navel

E. Pairing

was also referred to as the omphalos, an egg-shaped stone that was held in the innermost sanctuary at Delphi. Initially it was guarded by a large python, giving the place its original name, Pythos."

"There came a day when my brother Apollo slayed the python and it fell into a crevice in the earth. Over time Pythos became a holy site and was renamed Delphi after Delphyne the serpent. The dead snake that lay beneath it gave off fumes that had an intoxicating effect."

BR slowly turned the throne away from the table disappearing from view behind the chairs expansive back. In a matter of seconds it rotated back, a haggard old woman now taking the place of Artemis.

From behind the witch mask, BR continued her story in a deep, raspy tone.

"Within the enclosed inner sanctum dwelt an oracle, an older woman of blameless life who lived alone. People would make a pilgrimage to Delphi to consult the oracle about matters of utmost importance to their lives. She would enter a trance after inhaling the fumes from below. Apollo would become possessed by her spirit and convey her messages to the faithful."

The time to consult the oracle was determined from astronomical and geological grounds related to the constellations. The oracle could not be consulted during winter months. The oracle never gave a direct answer but spoke in allegories with hidden meanings and ambiguities.

"Now that sounds familiar," interjected Doc Holliday.

"To gain access to the oracle you first had to answer a riddle posed by the old woman."

"Now my dearies we come to an amazing coincidence. Delphi sits high up in a valley below two peaks."

"The peaks are known as Phaedriades, the breasts of Gaia. The overall layout of Delphi resembles a woman's body, complete with the breasts, the navel, and Delphi being known as the Vulva of Gaia."

"Fenn has tried to create the same image at the Jackson Hole site, with the fire pit and the Grand Tetons also representing a woman's body."

"Remember towards the end of the Chase Fenn gave what he called a mega-clue, saying "only a few are in tight focus with a word that is key". Well 'tight' is the shortest word you can have that includes the initials of The Grand Tetons. And now the best part, the region in Greece where Delphi is situated is named Phocis.

Do you recall Fenn's bizarre original story in TTOTC about flying over Philadelphia, get it Phila DELPHI a? He describes an incident late at night in his cockpit, where he clenches his left fist and hold it an inch in front of his eye, all the while watching the winking oxygen light down to the left of his hand.

I think this may be another method of identifying the treasure spot. The red winking oxygen light represents the firepit, as the chemical symbol for oxygen is O. The clenched fist creates a silhouette that matches the sky line of the Grand Tetons, the left thumb being the peak of Mount Teton. And the site of the treasure, and the navel of Gaia, is Fenn's heart pulse in his wrist, the same spot as the centre of the cross on the window.

Suddenly the witches eyes rolled back in her head, and voice from another world came with no movement of her lips.

"I see an old man in modern times who thinks he is Apollo. He delivers messages from another and has a riddle that must be answered before he will give up his wealth."

With this final flourish she collapsed, head down on the table.

Doc Holliday, Zorro, and Forrest Fenn himself sat in stunned awe.

"That's a hard act to follow," Zorro said, breaking the silence. "It certainly explains quite a few things in your writings Fenn."

"Yes, indeed, it all becomes quite obvious once the puzzle pieces are put together. But what is the word that is key?" he responded, staying perfectly in character.

"Only a few are in tight Phocis with a word that is key."

CHAPTER 23

BLOODLINES

Zorro took his place in front of the crushed velvet throne. Without bothering to sit he sprang to life. With an extravagant flourish he drew his sword and drew an imaginary Z in the air above the table.

"Careful with that thing Gringo, I may have to fill you with lead," warned Colt, removing his revolver from its holster, and placing it on the table.

"Good evening senores and senorita," he started in a broad Spanish accent, "I am Don Diego de la Vega. It is a peculiar thing to explain, gentlemen. The moment I don the cloak and mask, the Don Diego part of me falls away. My body straightens, new blood seems to course through my veins, my voice grows strong and firm, fire comes to me!, I become Zorro."

Dropping the accent, Tyler continued.

"The story I have to tell tonight is one of two F's – no, not Forrest Fenn, but family and friends. Everybody has family, in one form or another. For you Fenn, we know family was very special, but one member was more special to the Chase than all others. This is expressed subtlely in the photo on page 213 of TFTW, where your wife Peggy, and daughters Kelly and Zoe don't look happy to be having their picture taken. But the significance of the photo is not Peggy, Kelly, and Zoe. It is the X in the tree directly behind them, denoting the secret to finding the treasure is in your family tree. You then present a massive clue on the final pages of the same book, with a photo of your great grandparents, Nancy Elizabeth Davis and Edward Fix Davis. The clue here is in the middle names

Elizabeth and Fix. To solve it you have to have your eyes wide open. Fix becomes Fox, the translation of Zorro into English. And Elizabeth becomes ELOZABETH, an anagram of O THE BLAZE, the ring of fire."

"Fenn always said you had to find the blaze to find the treasure. In both the Ouray and Cody hunts the blaze was a person, Michael Blasie and Clayton Blaisdell Jr. And true to form, the blaze in the final hunt is also a person, your great grandmother Nancy Elizabeth Davis."

"It is fitting that she is at the end of the hunt as her initials are NED, an anagram for END."

"This is the END, my only friend, the End."

"Another ongoing theme throughout Fenn's books is the repetitive references to graveyards and grave markers. Is it possible we have to visit the grave site of Fenn's great grandmother to find out something relevant to the final solution. In one of his stories he deposits a nickel under the grave marker. Is it conceivable he has hidden something at her grave site to lead us to the end of the chase?"

"In genealogy and family trees the term great grandparents is often abbreviated to gg. Fenn uses this on a number of occasions to conceal major clues to the final scene. His continual reference to Piggy is a devilish clue placing his great grandmother (gg) at the final site, Py, short for Pythos or Pythia. Other members of his family are included in the closing scenario in a similar fashion. Peggy, representing the omphalus (egg) in Pythos (Py). Similarly Skippy, can be translated into peace (p's) in the sky."

Friends were equally as important to Fenn as family. So much so, he uses the noun 'friend' in most of his stories across the 3 books he produced in relation to the chase. Like everything else, there is a special reason for this. Not only does it emphasis the end, it also denotes the end is on Friday. The reason for this is not overly difficult to decipher. We began our quest in Jackson Hole on the first noel, the birth of Jesus Christ. It is only fitting we should finish on the day of his crucifixion, Good Friday, the day of his death on the cross.

My head was beginning to spin as these major revelations came thick and fast. Information overload was clearly not something Tyler was familiar with. He continued on without missing a beat.

"One of Fenn's close friends in Santa Fe was undoubtedly Val Kilmer, who played the man in black himself, Zorro, in the film The Mask of

E. Pairing

Zorro. Another of his acquaintances, George Hamilton, also played Zorro, in Zorro, The Gay Blade."

"Motherfucker", cried Colt, grabbing his six-gun from the table, "I warned you not to mention him again." With that he pulled the trigger, shooting Zorro square in the chest. Tyler flew backwards, dropping to the floor. Blood poured from the wound forming a puddle on the wooden floor beside his body.

"I guess the stage is all mine," said Doc calmly, standing up and shuffling across to the throne.

CHAPTER 24

JACKSON

Zorro crawled dramatically across the floor and pulled himself up into his chair.

With the audience now complete, Doc Holliday took a long slow draw from his tankard, emptying its contents down his throat.

"I'm in my prime," he drawled, spinning the tankard around his finger before placing it down on the table.

"Yeah, you look it," Tyler responded, reliving the famous Johnny Ringo scene from Tombstone.

You know what, you remind me of ………me," continued Doc, carrying on the re-enactment

"That's probably cause we're both Val Kilmer," joked Tyler.

"Were both Val Kilmer, smiled Doc, as he drew his gun from its holster and pumped another shot into Tyler.

Zorro slumped back in his seat, a fresh patch of blood appearing on his shirt.

"Fenn," Doc continued, turning his attention to me. "Your fascination with Val Kilmer is clear. It pervades all corners of the Chase. So many clues lead to my works. You once said that you were a maverick and understanding that was important to solving the chase. Everyone knows I was Iceman opposite Maverick in Top Gun, a movie that would have been intriguing to you as a former fighter pilot."

"Our homes in the hills outside Santa Fe are carbon copies of each other, filled with books, North American artifacts, and archaeological treasures.

E. Pairing

I also starred in The Island of Doctor Moreau, the cryptic answer to the TTOTC chapter Gold and More.

I was Moses in the Ten Commandments, parting the Red Sea.

I played the man in black in both the Batman Forever, and The Mask of Zorro.

I called my memoir, I'm your Huckleberry, taking the line from Tombstone, while also paying respect to Mark Twain

You even used my children, my dear daughter Mercedes, and my son Jack as key elements in your blessed hunt.

My part as Doc Holliday in Tombstone fitted perfectly with the themes of your Chase.

But more than anything my role as The Doors frontman Jim Morrison resonated with you.

Their music fits so well with the themes of the Chase. Come on Baby Light my Fire and Riders on the Storm.

But it was one song above all others that fitted into your master plan."

With this Colt leaned forward and tapped the play button on his phone with his revolver.

There was a momentary silence, then the music began.....

"This is the end, my only friend, the end........."

Doc left the phone playing and reached for the bottle of whiskey on the table, pulling the cork and filling his tankard. He lay back, drawing his hat down over his face, and sipping from the vessel every now and again while the 9-minute track played out.

On its completion he pushed the hat back up on to his head with the barrel of the gun and slowly opened his eyes.

Somehow he had miraculously transformed into The Joker.

"The second part of my ramblings is on a subject dear to my heart. Jackson, get it Jack son. A name littered throughout American history, making it so accessible for you to manipulate eh Fenn."

First, just for you Tyler, is my favourite connection. This man starred alongside me in True Romance. He was also known for his lead role in Shaft. Middle name Leroy, he was born in Washington DC, and became the second highest grossing actor of all time, Samuel L Jackson. Incredible given he has a stutter, a stutter, a stutter, a stutter he overcomes by using the word 'motherfucker' to get through his speech block.

Zorro moved nervously in his chair, with Artemis now clinging to his arm. Acknowledging the tension, Colt placed the mother-of-pearl-handled six-shooter he had been waving around down upon the table.

"My second Jackson connection," Colt announced, "is about the ice man himself - O'Shea Jackson Senior, better known as Ice Cube. He recorded the crudely titled song 'No Vaseline Motherfucker.'"

"But oh enough of this depravity, oops there goes gravity…"

The whiskey was taking over, and Doc was now channelling Eminem.

"My god, there are so many connections, but as Ice Cube once said, "In the end, it's just me and god"

"While those connections were a little tenuous, my third Jackson link is simply ingenious".

"Fenn," Doc announced, menacingly picking up his handgun from the table. "You chose Jack Stuef to bring your hunt to a close."

"Shortly after the treasure was found a photo was released showing you and 'The Finder' sitting in a motel in Santa Fe with the treasure spread out on a glass table in front of them. It was clearly posed. The head tilts of you and 'The Finder' are deliberately positioned to emphasise the similarities between you and him, the receding hairline, and strong European features. There is also the knowing look as you gaze into each other's eyes. There is a clear implication that there is a special bond between the two of you, supposedly through 'The Finder' discovering the treasure. Or is it perhaps to promote the fact you could be related?"

"A quick bit of research into The Finder's background and it doesn't take long to link him to you and the Chase. In 2012 he wrote for a magazine called The Awl. In OUAW you write a story about General John Bullis and an old Indian awl. Applying FennSpeak rules to Bullis and you have Bulls. The primary purpose of bulls being to sire progeny to extent the bloodline. Later in the story you dine at the bull ring just to emphasise the point. And the topic of The Finder's story in The Awl, sperm donorship."

"So is it possible 'The Finder' is actually related to you? That is the clear inference deliberately built into the story. While it is unlikely you are actually related, the clues are planted in such a way to give this impression."

"In TFTW you tell a story in Chapter 11, "Sun Valley Gig" about a summer he spent as a 19-year-old in Sun Valley managing a golf facility. You made extra money over-and-above your day pay by renting out the

E. Pairing

floor space in your room. You advertised it as "A floor and a bath for a buck and a half". Quoting directly from the story, "One cute brunette staked claim to a corner spot under the south window. When describing her there was no need to exaggerate." Fenn spent his twentieth birthday there, before being posted to the air force."

Applying Fenn rules to the story title, we get "sun valley gg", perhaps implying a link to a great grandson. Is it possible Fenn fathered a child that summer, and two generations later created a treasure hunt where is great grandson would be the beneficiary?

Jacks two F

Jacks FF

Jacks Forrest Fenn

How you came to bestow this honour upon a medical student from Boston is open to conjecture, however the letter you concocted with him is pure BS, littered with so many clues.

But the clue to surpass all others, the word 'crean'. You intimate Fenn loved unique words, such as the word crean.

What the hell is CREAN?

Well I'll enlighten you, for one, it is an anagram of NACRE

And NACRE = mother-of-pearl

And who was the mother of pearl? Nancy Elizabeth Davis of course. Pearl is your beloved grandmother, Fenn.

"Chose your words wisely," Colt demanded threateningly, brandishing his side arm drunkenly.

I stared down the barrel of the Colt 44. Colt had stolen my thunder somewhat and I didn't have a choreographed arrangement with him like he had with Tyler. Choosing defence as the best form of attack I went for the celebratory approach.

"A toast," I proclaimed, "to Pearl, my dear old nan".

"To Pearl," Colt responded, surrendering his gun once again to the table, and raising his tankard to the gathering. Artemis and Zorro responded, and we all drank to a woman we had never met.

Doc sank back into the throne, his message delivered. He stared across the table and gave the perfect lead-in line.

"Now what pearls of wisdom do you have for us Fenn."

Hidden bloodlines and the holy grail - this was all starting to sound like the plot to The Da Vinci Code, the 2004 best-selling book and subsequent movie by Dan Brown. The core premise of the story being the Holy Grail is not only a sacred chalice that held the blood of Christ, but also a representation of his bloodline. At the disgust of the Catholic church, it is claimed Jesus Christ and Mary Magdalene were husband and wife, and had a child. Christ's bloodline had then passed down through ensuing generations and was now in danger of being extinguished by the church to hide its existence. The symbol representing the chalice is a Y, which also symbolises a woman's womb. The symbol portrays femininity and fertility, the cup or vessel of humanity.

Fenn uses similar symbolism in his narrative. The letter 'I 'representing a prominent part of the male anatomy, while the letter 'O' denotes the opposing female form.

CHAPTER 25

THE PEACEMAKER

"Pearls of wisdom indeed, or maybe just pearls before swine," I added cynically, without trying to be insulting.

Under my straw hat, freshly clean shaven, in a check shirt, with wrap-around dark sunglasses, I must say, I looked remarkably like a 60-year-old Fenn.

Clutching a long garden hoe in one hand, and a plastic axe in the other, I began my dialogue.

"My time in Vietnam had a profound effect on me, fighting a war that was questionable at best."

"I hope my stories and the solving of my treasure hunt will leave an impression of me as a kind and generous man. And that some of the more salacious elements of the solution don't tarnish an otherwise glorious idea."

"More than anything I would like to be remembered as a Man of Peace."

"When I first set out to create the Chase I wanted it to be difficult but not impossible. I liken it to taking 4 large jigsaw puzzles, let's say 1000 pieces each, with no pictures on them, and mixing them in a box. Each piece being a clue in itself. Anyone entertaining the idea of solving the hunt would have to solve the clues attached to each piece, recognising the themes and patterns as they went. Slowly they would add a few pieces together and the pictures would start to form.

The Pearl Necklace

The Ouray hunt past Cutler Creek to Okeson Trailhead. Up and over into Winchester Gulch then back down into the valley of the Marble Cave to eventually discover the Camp Oven at the delta.

The Cody trail through Colters Hell, and on to Mummy's Cave. Up Clayton Mountain and back down to Castle Rock, before eventually finding the Rusty Key on the Axle Line. The realisation that every golf course has a Clubhouse, and this one at The Shooting Star looked out at one of the most magnificent sites on earth, The Grand Tetons.

It is here I can add some further detail.

You've identified my fetish for breasts, and the effect they have on me.

Rather naughty I know, given I said the Chase was child's play, but it was all just an intricate analogy about Peace, or should I say P's, one of my favourite letters.

The saying "I come in peace" features in many western scenes when the white man meets the Indians for the first time. But here it has a slightly different meaning.

In the wild west, the Peace maker was the single shot Colt 13-inch revolver handgun with a 7 ½ inch barrel. But I had my own peacemaker that was always close at hand. And when I come in peace (P's) it refers to pearls, as in the pearl necklace, a somewhat obscure slang term for the outcome of my fetish.

Also, within my extensive collection of North American artifacts one of my favourite pieces is Sitting Bull's peace pipe. But as has just been mentioned, I had a peace pipe of my own.

I could have constructed my hunt without this dalliance, but the temptation was too great as the pieces all fitted too snugly. The numerous quotes regarding peace are so apt for the final scene - here in the Grand Tetons at Xmas. 'Peace to all' is a case in point, a phrase found on so many Xmas cards, complete with idyllic snow-covered scenes. Then there's 'Rest in Peace' as this was to be my final resting place. 'Grace and Peace of God' is a little more obscure but is vital in connecting us with the spot where the end of the chase is played out.

As you know, each item I placed in the chest held special significance. The polished gold mirrors, the fetish necklace with the 39 amulets, the turquoise bracelet with the 22 stones set in it. So what was the importance of the small gold frog. For one, it looked more like a small penis than a frog, but there is also a connection to my Peace theme. You see, Peace Frog, is a song, by you guessed it, The Doors. It comes

E. Pairing

from their album, 'Weird Scenes Inside The Gold Mine', and the lyrics are based upon 3 poems written by Jim Morrison, and the theme of the poems – childbirth.

"But enough about Fenn's masterpiece," I continued, dropping the Fenn persona briefly. "I want to thank you guys for humouring an old man and coming along for the ride. The thought you have put into your presentations tonight was unbelievable. Together you have shed light on many of the defining elements to the Jackson Hole chapter."

"Briar-Rose, as Artemis you told a beautiful story overlaying Delphi and its surrounds on the Tetons. Greek history and its alphabet feature prominently throughout the Chase. You identified my Great Grandmother as the oracle. And also identified her correctly as the final Blaze. Originally you would have had to venture to her grave site to find the answer to the riddle. I have long since removed the solution, as grave tampering is a crime and a number of searchers had misinterpreted the clues and were digging around her final resting place.

Tyler as Don Diego de la Vega you then uncovered the critical theme relating to friends and having to complete the quest on Good Friday.

And finally Colt as Doc Holliday, you illuminated for us with some enlightening Jackson connections. You also revealed the thinly disguised announcement of the discovery of the treasure as being fabricated.

'The Finder' is in fact my replacement. That is why he is always referred to as the FINDER, an anagram of FRIEND.

…..as This is the End, my only Friend, the End….

You see, when you venture to the correct spot at the correct time on Good Friday, I was always there waiting. For nine years I made the trip to the spot and waited to no avail. If you could have ventured to the spot and answered the riddle, the treasure would have been yours. I would have given you a detailed map to where the treasure is buried. Without the map it could never be found.

Now that role has passed to the FINDER, my friend, he is the custodian of the treasure. On Good Friday he will be waiting at the spot. If you arrive on time and answer the riddle, the treasure will be yours.

I have to tell you how impressed I am you have come so far and so close to solving the Chase. The only things left for you to do is identify the correct time and place.

Oh yes, and to answer the riddle of course, 'As I have a long one'……. What is a long one to me?

The Pearl Necklace

Unfortunately I can't tell you the answer. It was many years ago and I have long forgotten.

Rather than give you the solutions to the time and place, I am going to give you a number of clues and hints, as some assistance to clear the final hurdle and to complete the ultimate quest.

1. The spot on the window of Room 4A highlighting the spot on the Grand Tetons does not point to the spot where I will be waiting
2. That spot is hundreds of miles from here
3. The spot is not in Wyoming, though the treasure was prior to being found
4. Rock is an important word

It turns out the Camp Oven and the Rusty Key didn't only give us CORK. It also is yet another anagram - ROCK.

When I said, 'you need to be in tight focus to discover a word that is key', the word was ROCK, derived from Rocky. As always, I can't be accused of not leaving some of the main clues in clear view for all to see.

5. GG stood for my Great Grandmother, but is also very important for other reasons, especially on Good Friday
6. Good is a word I like
7. The last line of the poem is vital. Remember to keep your eyes wide open all the time, and of course, follow my rules.
8. If you can solve these clues you will be very excited
9. The following puzzle could be useful in solving this final conundrum

There is an orchard with 9 pear-like trees in it, planted in a 3 x 3 square. Starting at the first tree, and walking in straight lines, visit each tree, making only 4 turns along the way.

Interpret these 9 clues correctly and you will know the time and place......but don't bother coming unless you know the answer to the riddle.

CHAPTER 26

THE END

The lounge area of Room 4 at the Antler Inn was an absolute tip. Clothes, bottles, and other debris was strewn from one end to the other. A large patch of tomato sauce still remained in a pool on the wooden floor, and a garden hoe was being used as a coat stand by the velvet throne. On the table were pieces of paper with workings and other scribblings on them, and in the throne lay Doc Holliday, fast asleep.

It was 10 o'clock and our flight to Denver was due to leave in 2 hours.

"Colt, time to rattle your dags," I demanded forcefully, as I walked across and banged on the bedroom door. "C'mon you guys, time to make tracks."

Eventually BR and Tyler appeared from the gloom, as I scurried around filling a garbage liner with the rubbish from the floor and table.

"How about you clean up the mess you and Tyler made during the shootout last night," I suggested, gesturing at the patch on the floor".

"It's his blood," Colt replied, "but I'll wipe it up."

"How did you guys get on with the hints after I went to bed? Did you find the spot?"

"We solved the pear tree puzzle, and made some other good connections, but didn't really agree on one distinct spot," answered Colt in a monotone that suggested his head was still foggy from the heavy night."

"You're just lucky we are going there today then," I replied, trying to inject some vigour into the group.

"What, in Denver?" said Colt, with a little more step in his voice.

The Pearl Necklace

"Fenn did say you'd find his car at the Denver Museum of Nature and Science. Pack your bags and we can talk about it at the airport and on the plane," I insisted.

Jackson Airport is the only airport in USA situated within a National Park. At 6,500 ft, its terminal is a beautiful, single level building resembling an expansive modern log cabin. It looks out at the majestic Grand Tetons.

After checking in our bags, we hunkered down in the lounge area to await our flight. I had been dying to know how the team had got on with the 9 clues from the night before.

"Ok guys, tell me how far you got," I enquired keenly.

"Not far, but too far to walk," confessed Briar-Rose. "It took us a while, but we solved the pear tree puzzle, and we think we know the significance of that. As for the rest, we have a few ideas, but they don't take us to any one special place."

"OK, tell me what you have, and I'll try and give you a few hints before we actually get there."

"The orchard puzzle is about thinking outside the square," confessed Tyler. "It is a classic puzzle that stymies people because they don't think to go beyond the points provided. So we're thinking this pertains to the spot on the window of Room 4A. The line from the spot on the window to the mountain carries on beyond the mountains identifying a point hidden behind the range, in this case we believe it to be Castle Rock, Idaho. After all, you said Rock was an important word."

"Yeah," joined in Colt eagerly. "Remember the story in OUAW, about the woman named Idah Meacham. Maybe that was a clue to the need to find a spot in Idaho. And it's only fair the 3rd stage of the Chase takes us to Castle Rock, as both the first two stages did the same. Only problem, we are now stuck in Idaho, which is not amongst Fenn's four chosen states.

"*Flight UAL1385 to Denver now boarding Gate 1,*" boomed the intercom.

"That's us," I declared, rising to my feet, slinging my satchel over my shoulder and heading for the gate. The other three followed suit, albeit sluggishly.

Once aboard the flight, we rekindled our conversation regarding the 9 clues. "So we've got Castle Rock. What else did you find?"

E. Pairing

"Well in Clue 5 you remind us GG stands for Great Grandmother, but it is also significant to Good Friday. If you study the story of Jesus's crucifixion you find some other interesting connections. For one, Jesus was put on the cross at Calvary. Calvary, just outside the walls of Jerusalem, is also known as Golgotha, GG, both names meaning the place of the skull. It is reputed that Jesus died around 3pm in the afternoon, and his body was taken down and taken to the Garden of Gethsemane, GoG. During this process a soldier pierced the side of Jesus, causing blood and water to gush forth. The weapon used has become known as the Lance of Longinus, which sounds like a name that would have tickled Fenn's fancy."

Also in the bible there is the character Gog, who appears in Revelations, at the End of Days, now known as the apocalypse. Given we are looking for where Fenn would like to die, this is probably significant."

"Then if we look at Good Friday, the word Good would have attracted Fenn's attention as he liked any word with double OO as it reminded him of the Grand Tetons, if you get what I mean. We looked at the background to the name Good Friday and discovered it derives from God Friday. And if you look at the last line of the poem, and apply the noel rule, gold becomes god!"

"My God, you guys are sooo close to cracking it," I enthused. "All you needed to do was open your eyes to the other clue in the last line of the poem and you would have had it."

"I've got my eyes wide open all the time," sang Tyler channelling Johnny Cash, and opening both his eyes as wide as possible.

Okay, this is the very last clue I am giving you.. it's the 'I' in title. I give you title...it's an anagram"

"U TOTLE, spelled out Briar-Rose methodically, "how about LET OUT?"

"God, let me out of here," expelled Colt loudly, causing the passengers around us to give some surprised sideways glances.

"Remember the end of the second trip, we spent our last day at The Outlet, at Castle Rock, just outside of Denver," I declared, deciding to put them out of their misery.

"No fucking way," expelled Tyler, causing more glances from the surrounding passengers, "Don't tell me, the treasure is in the Calvin Klein store."

The Pearl Necklace

"Closer than you think," I responded, "But remember that day. Because we spent so much time there, we didn't make it to the Garden of the Gods, by Colorado Springs."

"Get it, more double G, the G o G, the end of days."

"And look on a map and see what's just up the road from the Garden of the Gods. For one... the Eisenhower golf course, and two, right next door to that... the United States Air Force Academy.... Two places no doubt Fenn was very familiar with! And best of all, we are going there today."

It was mid-afternoon when the plane touched down in Denver. Out of deference to Fenn I had decided we would make the trip to the Gardens of the Gods from the Museum of Nature & Science. The cab ride from the airport was one of animated excitement. We were all aware that the trip from the Museum to Gardens would have been the same route Fenn would have taken during this final planning for the chase.

On arrival at the Museum grounds we immediately sought out the Grizzlies Last Stand statue, as it was felt this was another reason Fenn had chosen this as the site for one of his mega-clues. As far as statues go, it was attractive without being exceptional, though it did take us back to our own bear encounter up Cow Creek. After paying homage, we found the nearest bus stop and caught the next bus to the central bus station. From there we caught a ride to Colorado Springs, 70 miles to the south. Along the way, we past the Outlets at Castle Rock and the United States Airforce Academy. We also took the time to read up on the Garden of the Gods history. Interestingly the name Jackson featured strongly in its past, the most salient point being that the park had been named by Helen Hunt Jackson.

This reminded me of a humorous old story my father used to repeat when we were young. Whenever we were looking for something, he would tell us, the person in charge of lost property at the army barracks he served at was Helen Hunt, the punchline being, if you lost anything you should go to Helen Hunt for it.

Eventually we reached the Garden of the Gods, after catching a connecting shuttle from Colorado Springs. Our 3 hours on the bus had afforded us the opportunity to make a plan for our time at the park. We had read up on the spectacular red rock formations that were the dominant features in the landscape. Each had an intriguing name to

E. Pairing

match its shape or form, and these names were the perfect fodder for Fenn to mould into his concluding act. There were also other aspects of the park that provided deep connections with Fenn's creation. It was hard to ascertain which were the more meaningful.

Upon departing the bus at the Visitor Centre just outside the park, the distinctive fragrance of pinyon pine was readily apparent. Throughout his writings Fenn had waxed lyrical about the presence of this aroma at the final site. This was a major confirmation we were on the right path.

The afternoon was spent checking out the relevant features within the Garden of the Gods to evaluate their suitability to be the final rendezvous point of the Chase.

First there was the man-made stone circle aptly named the Jaycee Plaza. Given the central role Jesus Christ plays in the final scenario it was felt this was a strong candidate for the chosen last spot. Stone circles, Sir John Lubbock, the ring of fire, the flaming o. They all provided solid evidence to support this as the site Fenn would have selected to be waiting come Good Friday.

But it wasn't the only good option. Among the many huge red rock formations there was numerous contenders. They all had interesting names that could be linked to the Chase in some way.

Siamese twins, Pulpit Rock, the Tower of Babel, Toad and Toadstools, Steamboat, Sleeping Giant, Keyhole Window, Cathedral Spires. A case could be made for any one of them. But there were two that stood out above all the rest, the Three Graces, and the Kissing Camels.

It was four months until Easter. The merits of each of the potential candidates would be hotly debated because there could be only one winner.

The four months was also opportune. It gave be time to complete the first cut of this book and have it published. The reasoning for the book was simple. Thousands of people had been drawn in Fenn's vortex. The purported discovery of the treasure had only brought limited release. They were still tortured by not knowing the truth to where the treasure had been hidden, and the path to get there. Hopefully the book would provide at least some relief, together with the possibility the hunt was still alive.

CHAPTER 27

A LONG ONE

This time I had come alone, as the mission was a straight forward one – locate 'The Finder' within the Garden of the Gods, on Good Friday, at the time of Jesus's death, and deliver to him the answer to the riddle. In return I would receive directions to the treasure.

The flight from Melbourne to Denver via Honolulu had been a relaxing one. Over a few glasses of Sauvignon Blanc, I had studied my latest pre-occupation, The Hunt for the Golden Owl. There was a slight feeling of guilt, having moved on so quickly to a new mistress after spending 4 years in the clutches of The Chase. I promised myself this was just a light-hearted dalliance rather than the full relationship I had had with Fenn. I was yet to make any solid breakthroughs in regard to the new adventure, so the relationship was in its early stages and yet to get serious, or so I kept telling myself.

The plane touched down in Denver on Good Friday eve, just as the sun was disappearing behind the Rockies. After deboarding, I made my way to the baggage carousel. Everyone was jostling for position, and my bag was nowhere to be seen. I had tied a large piece of red ribbon to it to make it easier to recognise as it came around the conveyor.

After what seemed like an eternity, it appeared in the distance. Squeezing between two fellow travellers, I reached for the handle of the bag as it arrived in front of me. At exactly the same time another hand shot out and grabbed the handle. In unison the foreign hand and mine pulled the bag from the carousel and stood it up on the floor. I turned abruptly to confront the stranger attempting to take my luggage. He

E. Pairing

was a gentleman of similar age to me, and not dissimilar shape. He had a short goatee beard and was wearing a large Stetson and faded old blue jeans. His tee-shirt however was new, starchy white and had a quote in large black letters emblazoned across the front of it. I shuffled back slightly to get a clearer view of the message. 'As I have a long one' it read, above a large red question mark. It was in that moment I realised I may have created something bigger than ever anticipated, but for now I had to rescue my bag from Wild Bill's grasp.

"I think you have my bag," I said, trying to keep the mood as light as possible.

"I think you may be mistaken," replied Wild Bill gruffly, with some degree of confidence.

A sinking feeling overtook me, and I looked quickly down at the black suitcase sitting upright between us. Yes, it was very similar to my bag in that it was large and black, and sported an oversized red ribbon tied to the handle. However it also had a large name tag, with Frank Bender of Trenton, Pennsylvania written on it.

"I am so very sorry," I confessed, "I was sure this bag was mine."

In that instant, as if by magic, a second large black bag with red ribbon made its way along the conveyor. Scooping it off I set it down beside its twin.

"Great minds think alike," said Wild Bill dryly. "Are you here for the Friendboree?"

"Wouldn't miss it for the world." I replied, making it up as I went along, as I had no idea what the stranger was talking about. "Got my riddle solve locked in," I said, tapping the side of my head with my forefinger.

"How are you getting to Colorado Springs? Do you want to hitch a ride with this good ol'boy? We can swap notes on the way."

"Sounds perfect, I'll just need to cancel my rental," I replied as we pulled up the bag handles and headed for the car rental stands. "Where are you staying?"

"The Garden of the Gods Resort of course, where else."

The drive to Colorado Springs was enlightening. Wild Bill filled me in on the Friendboree, something I was blissfully unaware was going on. It transpired there had been extensive media coverage locally about The Pearl Necklace, The End, and the Good Friday riddle theory. It was predicted there would be upwards of 10,000 people venturing to The

The Pearl Necklace

Garden of the Gods tomorrow to stake their claim to the treasure. The old Fennboree crowd had organised a ball at the Garden of the Gods Resort tonight as one last event to mark the end of the Chase. It was fancy dress, come as your favourite Fenn character. 'The Finder' had come out publicly and said he wouldn't be attending. Nor would he be at the riddle answering gig at the Gardens the following day. In keeping with the riddle theory, and to ensure everyone attending had a chance to still submit their answer, the authorities were setting up a large letter box within the stone circle in the garden, as this seemed to be the favoured spot to most of the attendees. They were even offering a $5,000 prize for the most original answer, as well as numerous other spot prizes.

Eventually the conversation moved to the riddle. I had the feeling since we had left the airport Wild Bill was dying to try his answer out on me.

"I'll show you mine if you show me yours," he said with a smile.

"Not a happening thing," I responded, "anyway I haven't made my final decision," I lied.

"No worries, I might try mine on you anyway," Wild Bill chuckled.

There were a few minutes silence before out of the blue Wild Bill blurted out "Nose."

It certainly wasn't one of the options I had considered and came as a bit of a surprise. Not wanting to burst his bubble I played along,

"Well, who…knows, you could be right," I offered up jokingly.

"Exactly," Wild Bill responded, "but it's much cleverer than that. I'll explain. You know Apocalypse Now, and This is the end. My only friend, The end.

"How could I not," I replied, thinking to myself, if only this guy knew the truth.

"Anyway, everyone knows Fenn wrote most of that book. And one of his rules was using short words like not, nod, and now, as in Now meaning no 'W'.

"What does that have to do with having a big nose?" I enquired.

"Bear with me," Wild Bill continued, pushing his Stetson back a little.

"W stands for west, so no west, only North South, and East. Then you add in O for the final site, the ring of fire, and you have nose. Fenn always said there was two scents to follow. So all you needed to follow to find the treasure was your nose.

E. Pairing

I was now starting to doubt my own solution that I had flown half way around the world to deliver.

"Brilliant," I said genuinely, as Wild Bill swung the Jeep Wrangler into the Garden of the Gods Resort carpark.

"See you in the bar at 7 o'clock for a pre-ball drink," Wild Bill shouted out as we departed reception for our accommodation.

My room was comfortable with views out over the gardens, though it was quite dark outside now. The huge rock formations that dominated the park formed spectacular silhouettes against the moonlit sky. This was paradise, but I had a dilemma. The Friendboree had come as a surprise, and I didn't have a costume for the ball.

Looking through my bag I managed to find a check shirt and my old jeans. I had also packed my straw hat, and had my wraparound sunglasses with me, so a pretty plain looking Forrest Fenn it was. I figured there would be a few other Fenn look-alikes there and I would go completely unnoticed.

The plan worked perfectly. On entering the bar I was encountered by a sea of men in black. There was a few Agent J & K's from the movie, as well as a High T, Batman, and Zorro's galore, and or course, a couple of Johnny Cash's. There was even a man in black from the Dark Tower. The more creative had dressed up as characters from Fenn's books such as Sosoko, Quanah Parker, Chief Ouray, and Buffalo Bill. If anything there was more woman than men in the crowd, and their costumes were more imaginative, due to the shortage of female characters within Fenn's literature. There was even a couple of Denim Roses, that gave me a personal thrill.

I scanned the room for Wild Bill. It took a while, but I managed to spot him at the far end of the bar. He hadn't told me he was coming as Zorro, so I was relieved to have picked him out. Shuffling through the crowd, I reacquainted myself with my new friend over a couple of cold ones.

The Ball was being held in the dining room next door. It had been cleared of tables and chairs, and was dimly lit, creating a marvellous spectacle, as the huge, curved windows along one side of the spacious room gave a magnificent vista out onto the gardens. Lights had been strategically placed at the bottom of the huge red rock features, giving the gardens an out-of-this-world appearance.

At precisely 9 o'clock the music stopped and the room gradually fell silent. The helicopter scene from Apocalypse Now lit up the big screen on the back wall and the thunderous roar of the choppers played in surround sound, before gradually fading into 'The End' by The Doors.

"This is the end, my only friend, the end....."

The hair on the back of my neck stood on end and my hearted pounded as I gazed around the room.

I looked over at Wild Bill. He gave me a sly wink and tapped the side of his nose.

Suddenly a spotlight beamed down from the ceiling, and a figure stepped into it holding a cordless microphone. Surprisingly, he was dressed as The Joker.

"Welcome my friends to the show that's about to end," he shouted as if introducing a world title fight. "Tomorrow someone in this room is very likely to become the owner of the fabled Fenn treasure." In a slickly choreographed move the chest and its golden contents appeared on the screen behind him, and the room gave out a collective gasp. "I wish each and every one of you good luck. All you have to do is identify what Fenn was talking about when he said, As I have a long one? Honestly, how hard can it be?"

"Just to be clear. If there is more than one penis in the box tomorrow, and it is judged to be the best answer, we will put them all in a hat and draw one out at random. If your name is pulled out, the $5000 will be yours." The well lubricated crowd erupted with laughter and loud chatter.

Once order was restored, the Joker then moved on to presenting a number of prizes including 'best costume'. The award went to Gary Player in his black attire, complete with his golf trundler and clubs as well as his wife and six children, all dressed in matching tartan outfits. I thought to myself, I hope the prize was worth the effort.

With the formalities done, the music kicked back into life and the party returned to its former rowdiness. I don't know if it was the fancy dress, or the shared vision amongst the group, but the atmosphere was uninhibited, bordering on out of control. Moving about the room everyone was having a good time. At one stage I came upon a comely woman decked out as Charmay Allred, complete with red dress and feathered headpiece. I recognised her instantly from her picture in TFTW.

E. Pairing

"Forrest, you old charmer," she gushed, embracing me tightly like a long, lost friend.

"The answer I already know," she whispered into my ear, before drawing away, giving me a wink as she did so. It suddenly dawned on me the relevance of that line from the poem. Once again I began second guessing my answer to the riddle.

As the party continued I made many new friends and drank a few too many beers.

Well after midnight, the music stopped, the lights came up and the big screen displayed the words, 'This is The End...' in a half circle around a picture of Fenn. There was a loud cheer from the crowd, as 'American Pie' began blaring from the speakers. As one, the crowd began to sing along, hugging and kissing each other as if there was no tomorrow.

"....... and singing this with be the day that I die, this'll be the day that I die."

The noise was deafening, and I found myself with my arm around two total strangers. As the lyrics scrolled across the bottom of the screen, I began seeing patterns in the words, ...whiskey, could that be the word that is key.....?

I knew it was time to leave. I gingerly weaved my way through the crowd toward the door exiting through the bar. Once outside, I looked to the heavens. It was a clear night, and the stars were out. As I struggled to find the Hunter constellation, it dawned on me, today was the day. Four long years of hope and obsession were going to come to an end. I thought of the team back home and their hopes for finding the treasure. Wandering the short distance back to my room I took comfort in the fact I could sleep in until late in the morning. The prevailing school of thought for timing on Good Friday was centred around the crucifixion of Jesus. While much controversy surrounds the timing of Jesus's death, it is generally accepted he was put on the cross at 9am, and breathed his last at 3pm in the afternoon. Following this line I intended to not rise until after midday.

Making my way into the gardens through the carpark I was met by a group of protesters waving banners and placards. 'Respect the holy day' a woman dressed in a purple tie-died kaftan shouted at me as I tried to sneak past unnoticed. A young girl shoved a large homemade sign with 'Work this out – 'Blas 4 me' scrawled upon it into my face. Sidestepping her I quickened my stride and made for the path down to Jaycee Plaza.

The track was crowded. It seemed most people had decided to come around 3pm although the box for depositing the riddle answers in had been there all day. There was a rumour circulating you still had to deliver the correct answer at the correct time to collect the treasure. The rumour also implied the treasure was actually up for grabs and that the Finder had negotiated with the organisers to record the whole event to identify the identity of anyone inserting the exact answer at the right moment.

The closer I got to the plaza the more chaotic the scenes were becoming. People still dressed in their costumes from the previous night were jostling and pushing each other to get to the box fixed to the ground in the middle of the stone circle. Security guards were doing their best to keep control but were fighting a losing battle. As I skirted around the outer edge of the area scuffles were breaking out ...

I headed down the path to the 3 Graces. My gut told me The Finder would honour his promise to Fenn and make an appearance. The path to the Graces and the area around it were packed. People clearly felt Fenn would have wanted to die with his family and were following that hunch.

Thinking this was a little too obvious for Fenn I threaded my way through the hordes and found the path around to the Kissing Camels.

The crowd was thinner and more subdued as it consisted mainly of those who had cast their guesses into the bin and were now making the most of the cloudless day scrolling around the park.

Reaching the Camels arena I checked my watch. It was 5 minutes to 3.

As I approached the massive rock formation, I noticed a middle eastern gentleman dressed in long robes and a turban, standing in the shadow of the kissing camels. It seemed odd he would be here as his costume didn't match anyone from Fenn's literature.

I looked across and caught his eye and instantly knew it was him. He looked into my eyes and knew it was me.

There was a brief, uncomfortable pause, then I reached into my jacket pocket and pulled out a blank entry form.

With a pen I'd retrieved from my shoulder bag I scribbled on the paper in the gap designed for the answer.

E. Pairing

It read,

As I have a long .....

'LIFE LEFT TO LIVE'

I handed it to him, and he read it slowly. Showing no emotion, his eyes staring blankly into the distance, he screwed the piece of paper into a ball and dropped into the rubbish bin beside him. He then extended his left hand toward me from under his robes. His fist was in a ball face down, making it clear he had something to give me. I placed my open hand under his and felt the weight of a small object as it dropped into my palm. I knew immediately what it was, as, though small, it was very heavy for its size. Looking quickly down to verify its form I could see it was the small gold frog.

In this moment I realised it had never been about the treasure, only a quest to find the truth. A massive weight lifted off me and a state of euphoria overtook my mind and body.

I turned and walked slowly away toward the path leading back to the 3 Graces. I thrust my hand into my right-hand pocket screwing up the piece of paper remaining there. As I passed the rubbish bin beside the path I furtively pulled out my hand and dropped the ball of paper into it.

In my head, the music began playing....

This is the end, my only friend, the end

CHAPTER 28

GONE ALONE

Back into my room at the resort I gently placed the golden frog down on the glass topped table and dialled Australia. It was getting late into the night there, but I knew the team would still be up waiting to hear the outcome of the day.

"What made you chose the Kissing Camels?" enquired Briar-Rose eagerly.

"A number of small things really, like, just maybe, CK stood for Camels Kissing. Also the camels fit the hot, dry landscape of the gardens, the scene for Jesus's crucifixion, and the three wise men and all that."

"Nice," congratulated Colt.

"But then there was a bigger realisation. Something I had suspected for ages. That Fenn's affection for animals was maybe more than just emotional."

In the TTOTC Fenn tells a story about his pet calf Bessie. The story highlights a number of key elements of the Chase.

The first of these is relatively straight forward. The name Bessie is a short form of Elizabeth, and ELIZABETH, once the 'I' is removed is an anagram of THE BLAZE.

The second clue is the reference to giving each of six kittens, five squirts of milk each. This is a hint at the well-known, old-time 'As I was going to St. Ives' riddle', hinting there is a riddle to be answered.

The third element is Fenn's confession of his love for his pet calf.

E. Pairing

Fenn's attraction to animals is more blatantly portrayed in TFTW where he intimates that if you let his donkey Buttercup suck your finger he will follow you up to the bedroom.

It had dawned on me, these far-fetched stories were referencing an age-old joke. One that is even more unacceptable today than in the days when it was more popular.

Why are camels known as the ships of the desert?

"I've heard this one," Colt blurted out, "They are filled with Arab semen."

BR rolled her eyes, "You guys will never change," she chastised.

"I get it," Tyler chimed in, looking up from his Sudoku. "Kissing Camels. Not so much camel kissing camel, but something else, like lonely Arabian nights."

"These two clues, one hinting at a riddle, the other at a joke, also point to another overarching theme – The Riddler and The Joker, both adversaries of Batman, the man in black. Throughout the chase Fenn sees himself as both, with riddles and jokes being key to the solution."

"There is the ever-present question of whether the clues are taking us toward the treasure or leading us up the garden path as they say."

I had always suspected the more salacious elements to the chase may have been an enormous smoke screen. Fenn implies this in a story in TFTW about a time he was delivering milk. He ran into a house and surprised a spinster ironing totally naked save for a pair of earrings and some rouge. There is the clear implication here that these type of stories are red earrings, get it, red herrings.

Reality then descended upon me.

Each of the features in the Garden of the Gods had pros and cons for being the final spot. Some were based upon the more sordid facets of the chase, while others the more wholesome aspects. It was the age-old battle between good and evil, black and white, fidelity and infidelity, heaven and hell, god and the devil.

It was unlikely Fenn would have chosen the Kissing Camels as the final destination given the background we were now aware of. Surely Fenn would have chosen the good and righteous route for the finale.

The euphoria of the last hour drained away, and the feeling of déjà vu overtook me. It was the end of the Ouray chase all over again. Forrest Fenn had led me down a deep rabbit hole and left me stranded there. We may have come into possession of the golden frog, but our path to the truth had been a side-track inhabited by demons from the underworld. I picked up the frog and examined it closely. Scratching it with my thumbnail it became immediately apparent the figurine wasn't gold at all but lead with gold paint upon it. It felt like a scene out of a Sherlock Holmes movie, where the evil Moriarty had outfoxed his arch-rival once again.

Not for the first time, the flight back to Australia was a long ride home. The entire plane trip was spent playing every angle of the chase back through my mind. There were still a few loose pieces of the puzzle not connected....were they the secret to finding the solution?

It took most of the journey, and a few glasses of sauvignon blanc but it finally came to me. And it came via the strangest of ways.

After sifting through all the remaining loose ends, and there were many, I thought maybe, just maybe, I could use backward engineering to find the solution. The answer to the riddle might be a clue to the final solution.

My riddle solve consisted of two words, made up of critical aspects of the chase, each with eleven letters. 11/11 I thought – the date of two significant events each year, two events that illuminate the reason Fenn chose the Garden of the Gods as the backdrop to the final scene. It wasn't specifically the Garden of the Gods, but their proximity to Castle Rock and the Airforce Academy.

Firstly there is Veterans Day, commemorating the end of the war to end all wars, World War 1. When the armistice was signed at the 11th hour, of the 11 day, of the 11th month, 1918. Each year Fenn would try and make it back to the Academy to mark this day and pay respects to past and present servicemen and women.

Then there is Singles Day, more commonly referred to as Black Friday (although 11/11 only falls on a Friday every 7th year). It is a day/week marked by massive retail sales, and a key event for malls such as The Outlet at Castle Rock.

Long before becoming popular in the USA, Singles Day had originated in China. 11/11 was chosen, as the numeral 1 represents a bare stick, which is Chinese internet slang for an unmarried man who does not add branches to his family tree.

It suddenly dawned on me the significance of the first line of the poem....As I have gone alone in there.......it was a direct reference to singles day....

E. Pairing

and there within the words the two ones ....**gone** a**lone**.

How the hell had it taken me four years to realise the significant of something I had discovered on day 1?

Some of the unconnected pieces now started to fall into place.

Baby Face Nelson, the solution to Chapter 11 'Totem Café Caper' in TTOTC, came to the fore. It is a tough answer for Americans to interpret but for solvers in the cricket playing countries of the world it is a little easier. In cricket the number 111 is nicknamed Nelson, named for Lord Nelson who reputed died having only one eye, one arm, and one leg, although this isn't entirely true as he still had both legs at the time of his death.

Was the Nelson suggestion also an oblique reference to the fact Fenn only had two daughters and nil sons. I guess we will never know.

There is another reference to Johnny Cash is all of this. In 2001 Cash produced an album, American 111: Solitary Man. On it he sings a duet with his good friend, Willy Nelson.

Fenn's ultimate finale was now fully uncovered. It was the perfect scenario. Each November he could travel with the family to Denver on the 10th. Next morning Peggy and the girls could be dropped at The Outlet for the Black Friday sales. Fenn could then venture to the Garden of the Gods. Making his way through the hot red rock features, he would arrive at the 3 Graces just prior to 11am. There he would wait for the successful solver to come with the answer to his riddle. For nine straight years he had made this journey in vain, waiting in front of the 3 towering rocks resembling the number 111, with the shadows between them spelling out the number 11. They were the ultimate embodiment of what the chase was about – light and shadow, good and evil, fidelity and infidelity, white Christmas, and Black Friday. They also resembled an enormous fire, the final blaze.

Each year Fenn had left slightly deflated that no one had unravelled his devious masterpiece. No one had turned up to the chosen spot at the designated time. Disappointed he would then make his way to the Air force academy just up the road to commemorate Veterans Day and reconnect with his former military buddies.

In 2019, with failing health, and increasing pressure from all angles he devised another cunning plan. He would bring the curtain down on the Chase by orchestrating the discovery of the treasure. In doing so he would take the heat off his family after his passing.

Only those with intimate knowledge of Fenn Speak would realise he had merely transferred the custodianship of the treasure to someone else who would make the annual pilgrimage to the 3 Graces to await the most dedicated of hunters. Even then the treasure would not be theirs. They would still need to deliver the answer to the ultimate riddle.... As I have a long one?

And so it was, the chase was still alive. A return trip to Denver for the Cisco team was back on the agenda. What was another $15,000 when we had already invested $85,000?

CHAPTER 29

BLACK FRIDAY

The seven months between Good Friday and Black Friday took an eternity to pass.

Briar-Rose and Tyler got engaged and were getting married in late November. They busied themselves making the arrangements for the wedding of the year. No expense was spared, as there was a possibility we would be $2M richer, although we no longer spoke with the certainty we had in the past. Colt was also in a serious relationship, and was more attached to his new girlfriend than the tenuous chance of acquiring new wealth. Heather hadn't changed her views on the Fenn treasure hunt, and the other two siblings had progressed well in their chosen careers over the 4 years we had been chasing the dream. One was now representing her country at football, while the younger of the two was half way through a law degree and the senior mooting champion at the local university.

In the end it was decided I would go alone again, in keeping with the poem. There was a risk in this approach, in that I could only be in one spot at the prescribed time. It was unanimously decided this would be The 3 Graces. Representing Peggy, and his two daughters Kelly and Zoe, the 3 giant pinnacles of red rock symbolised the wholesome half of the Fenn's masterpiece. They were also a physical representation of the ultimate blaze. And then there was the riddle. They fitted in nicely with the 2 x 11 letter solution and its derivation. But over and above all this, The 3 Graces was the solution to my all-time favourite clue. It is the photo on page 213 of TFTW, with Peggy, Kelly, and Zoey sitting in front of the tree with the X in it. The photo could easily be titled 'The 3 Grim Faces'. If we remove the IMF from the title, for the family member not present, 1 M----- F-----, we are left with The 3 Gr(im f)aces.

It was winter again when I touched down at Denver Airport. This time my black bag with its large red ribbon was the only one like it on the carousel. There was not the excitement of the previous visits to recover the treasure. The let-downs of the past had deflated the tyres somewhat and I was more hopeful than optimistic this time around.

Arriving at my motel in Colorado Springs, it was bustling with veterans catching up with their comrades before their biggest day of the year tomorrow. I kept a close eye out for another individual who might also be there for a specific rendezvous tomorrow, but to no avail.

Next morning it was Friday. This was a good omen. The 11th of the 11th only occurred on Friday every 7 years, disregarding the impact of leap years, so it truly was Black Friday. It was 2 degrees Celsius outside. This certainly didn't fit with the middle eastern, hot red rock theme of the Garden and it's Kissing Camels.

Rugging up in a long coat and scarf, I made my way to the bus station. It was 9 o'clock when the shuttle departed, with only a scattering of people on board. I also took this as a good sign, meaning it was unlikely someone else had solved the Chase and was making their way to the Garden to lay claim to the prize. On the other hand, the finder wasn't on the bus either, meaning he had either made his own way to the park or was coming on a different shuttle.

After the bus had pulled into the visitor centre I wasted no time in heading toward the 3 Graces. The park was very quiet with only a sprinkling of tourists checking out the amazing scenery. I was early, but wanted to get into position to survey the lie of the land. Heading down the Gateway Trail I pondered on how different it was to the last time I had been here. It was summerish then and the park was overrun by the crazies. Now there was a light layer of snow on the ground and only a few people about. I checked my watch, 10:15. Plenty of time to skirt around past Jaycee Plaza and make my way to the 3 Graces.

Approaching the colossal rock structure, I admired Fenn's choice of this as the final blaze. It resembled a giant fire rising up from the frozen earth. Convinced I was now in the right space at the right time, I began looking around for 'The Finder'. Surely he would be here early as well.

10:30 No one

E. Pairing

10:45 A couple of random tourists taking selfies with the 3 Graces in the background

10:55 No one

11:00 Still no one

11:11 A loved-up honeymoon couple wandering along the path.

I was starting to despair. It was now 11:20 and still no sign of Two F's.

A message pinged up on my phone. It was Colt.

"Check out Heritage Auctions Texas!"

I opened my browser and hurriedly cut and pasted Colt's message into it.

Instantly the first search response flashed onto the screen,

"Bidding now open on Forrest Fenn's famed treasure."

My heart dropped into my boots. WTF, this couldn't be true?

Hurriedly, I began reading the blurb below the headline. It explained how The Finder had sold the treasure to a third party, Tesouro Sagrada Holdings LLC, several months ago, and now 476 individual lots were being auctioned, with advance bidding beginning today, the 11th of the 11th.

Was this a 1 in 365 coincidence, or a premediated act? My mind was working overtime.

I began scrolling down through the items. They were all there, the golden frog, the fetish necklace, the 20,000-word autobiography in the olive jar, the egg-sized nuggets, and hundreds of gold coins. Almost everything, bar the dragon bracelet and the treasure chest itself.

It was only then I realised I was a year too late. Fenn had probably agreed for The Finder to venture to the park for two years after his passing. If the treasure was unclaimed after that time, it was his to do with what he pleased. It dawned on me, one year previous would have been the 11th day of the 11th month 2021, 11 years after Forrest Fenn had set the Chase in motion. Had that day been the last opportunity to answer the riddle and claim the treasure?

Reverting back to the cell phone screen, I noted the auction for the treasure was in a month's time. Scrolling through the items, I tried to gauge my feeling towards them. Strangely, most of them had lost their appeal completely. The coins were packaged in plastic covers and looked like any other coins in a numismatic auction or shop. When they had been together in the chest in an unknown location in the great outdoors they held a strong emotional attraction. Now they were sitting in a catalogued box in an auction house, they meant nothing to me. The

The Pearl Necklace

printed labels on them, signifying they were part of the Forrest Fenn Treasure, did little to change that perception.

Only the small golden frog and the autobiography in the olive jar had any emotional impact. Each held a special significance to me. Sadly, even the fetish necklace had lost its appeal.

The 20,000 words, written so small it would take a magnifying glass to read them, and stored for 12 years in the sealed glass jar, would hopefully provide validation to the final solution. The interpretation of the events and stories throughout Fenn's life are open to conjecture, and the autobiography would shed intimate light onto their true meaning. All those now conversant in Fenn Speak would have recognised the significance of the words being kept in an olive jar. For those still struggling with this encoded language, O Live, a final reminder to this aspect of Fenn's life. Placing a value on this item is difficult. There was a number of contentious questions surrounding the item. Had the seal on the jar been compromised and the contents copied? Was there any guarantee there was a 20,000 autobiography on the enclosed paper (the description of the item had been changed to include the word 'purported' autobiography, to absolve the auction house of any liability should the paper be blank, or unreadable)?

The small gold frog had always been the single item I took to symbolise the Fenn treasure. The fact it represented a small, golden penis was irrelevant to that assessment. I had always strategized that after finding the treasure I would create another hunt using the frog as the centre piece of the treasure, hoping it would come to hold special significance amongst the armchair treasure hunting community.

My emotions were in a spin as I retraced the route and made my way back to my motel in Colorado Springs. The ball game had changed, and I needed to concoct a new strategy. It was clear my $100,000 investment to-date was not going to lead to a $2M windfall. The treasure was now freely available to all, provided they were the highest bidder. I looked at the items of interest, estimated the significance of obtaining them, and worked out the sum I was willing to pay.

It quickly became apparent over the next few days, as I travelled back to Australia, the price for the small gold frog was going to escalate well beyond my budget. At 28.8g in weight, the gold value was about $US 1700. The advance bidding was already above $US 8,000. The historic

E. Pairing

and recent significance of the item were well known but the projected sale price in advance of $US 30,000 was extreme.

After discussion with the team, the decision was made. Rather than split the budget between the two items, we would focus on just one, the 20,000-word autobiography. We hoped the addition of the word 'purported' to the item description in the sale catalogue might confirm peoples reservations regarding the completeness of the autobiography and put them off bidding.

Potentially it held the answer to the two remaining missing puzzle pieces;

1. Where had the treasure been hidden for the 10 years before it was discovered?
2. Was The Finder actually linked to Fenn via a liaison he had had many years prior?

Our greatest fear was we could be bidding for an item with little-to-no worth. Taking into account everything we had discovered to-date about Fenn and his master plan, it would come as no surprise for the scroll of paper within the olive jar to be blank. This would fit in perfectly with the suspicion of many that the whole affair was a hoax.

We figured, if we were luckily enough to secure the autobiography, it would confirm our solution to the chase and give credence to our story. If the manuscript was blank, no one would know, and it would also make our story appear genuine.

The day of the auction finally rolled around. It was late evening in Texas, so the middle of the next day in Melbourne, Australia. The team had all taken the afternoon off work and had gathered in the war room to witness what would most likely be the final act in our quest for the Fenn Treasure.

Logging in to the Heritage Auction site, they were already well into the catalogue of items.

The fetish necklace had sold for a whopping $US 46,800, and the gold frog had just been knocked down for $US 38,400.

The speed of the auction was breath-taking, each lot being sold in a matter of minutes, with both live and on-line bids coming in at lightning speed. It appeared everybody wanted a piece of the action, and they were willing to pay over the odds to secure it.

The Pearl Necklace

We joked around and drank a few beers while we waited for our target lot to appear. It was the last on the ticket, lot 476. Before long they had reached Lot 475. It was a pair of rusty old scissors that had been found in the chest with the treasure. Supposedly they had been accidently left in the chest by Fenn. As with all thing Fenn, this is unlikely. The scissors are in keeping with the solution to the chase, their shape mirroring the female form. The double O finger holes symbolising a pair of large breasts, the lower Y design, a woman's torso and long legs. When the breasts are pushed apart, the legs also open up, transforming the Y into an X. Could Fenn have placed the scissors in the chest as final verification that the treasure had been hidden at the site that was at the centre of rumours for the latter years of the Chase. It had been theorised on-line and even featured in Daniel Barbarisi's book, 'Chasing the Thrill', as the potential resting place of the chest. It was suggested the place that was so very special to Fenn was the spot he had first had intimacy with a woman. Is it conceivable (pardon the pun) that this is how The Finder worked out where the treasure was hidden?

In a matter of minutes the rusty pair of $10 scissors had been sold for the handsome sum of $US 2880. I started to wonder at the value of the camp oven we had left in the bush just outside of Ouray.

The last item on the card was Lot 476, the 20,000-word autobiography in the sealed olive jar. We had set aside the ridiculous sum of $US 25,000 to secure the item. We were on the edge of our seats as the activity kicked off.

The action began at the pre-bidding sum of $19,000 and rose past our budget figure in the blink of an eye. Within minutes the bidding frenzy saw the price surge past $40,000 before finishing at the grand figure of $US 48,000, bringing the overall auction to an end.

We looked at each other like stunned mullets. Not for the first time there was a deep feeling of disappointment. We had become accustomed to these anticlimactic let-downs. If nothing else, the Chase had taught us to pick ourselves up after adversity and move on to the next challenge.

After a brief autopsy of what went wrong, Briar-Rose and Tyler departed. Colt stayed on and we talked about this and that for a while. Suddenly he looked down at his watch and declared he had a surprise for me. I was surprised, as it was not like Colt to be spontaneous.

CHAPTER 30

THE DEMOSTHENES SEQUENCE

Colt leapt up and turned the large screen TV on before flicking off the room lights on the way back to his seat. He then somehow synced the screen to his phone. A crypt-like room came into view on the screen. In the darkened room there were people seated around a circular stone table, but the blackness of the scene and the darkness of our room, made it difficult to make out. It was like one of those annoying movies where it is so gloomy you struggle to follow the plot. Just as my anxiety levels were rising, a match was struck, and a small candle lit in the middle of the table. It illuminated the scene sufficiently to reveal seven characters dressed like monks positioned evenly around the wheel. The dark habits complete with cowls made it impossible to distinction the identity of the participants.

"Good afternoon Earl," came a deep voice from the under one of the hoods. It sounded vaguely familiar, but I couldn't put a face to the voice. The speaker reached up under their chin and unfastened a clasp, allowing the habit and cowl to fall away, revealing an immaculate black tailored suit. And there in the darkness was the unmistakable figure of Denim Belle. "Welcome my friends," she quipped with a broad grin.

I was taken aback. I looked across at Colt. He was all business, staring intently at the screen.

"It is great to see you again. Let me introduce my fellow staffers from the Order 322", stated DB with a high degree of formality.

The Order 322. I was immediately in shock. Throughout the chase there had been hints at a connection to the Order 322 – The Skull & Bones Society, but I'd always suspected they were a back story, to bring intrigue and atmosphere to the hunt. Surely they weren't actually involved.

"Firstly, I'm certain you will remember this trio," announced DB. In a similar routine to previous, they unbuttoned their habits and let them fall away to the floor. The eye-patch was an immediate give-away. It was the two barmen from the roof-top bar in Ouray, also dressed immaculately in the all-black suits. Beside them sat the unmistakeable figure of Snoop Dogg 2, the purveyor of fine weed from the Fiddler's Green. He cut an impressive figure in the black uniform complete with silver skull and bones lapel badge of the order.

"God I would love one of those," I thought to myself.

"Next," continued DB, "are your old friends Bindi-Anna and Darian." Both giving a peace sign as their gowns dropped away.

"And finally we have Bill Bison, thankfully fully attired on this occasion." He responded with a broad smile and a wink.

"You are undoubtably wondering how we are all together in the same room." After a pause for contemplation, DB continued. "Together we were the gate keepers to the entrance to the Chase. It had been designed by our colleague Fenn to be near impossible to solve without coming through the front portal."

"For twelve long years we worked as a group to oversee the activity at the entranceway. Together with our online operatives we monitored those who had solved the front-end clues and were venturing up into the wilderness north of Ouray."

"Incredibly, in that time, of the small number of searchers who ventured into the area, only one incursion managed to find the Camp Oven 'false' treasure. And on that occasion it was only condoned due to the precise instructions provided by you to B & D. Unfortunately that

E. Pairing

event took place immediately prior to the pre-ordained termination of our programme."

"No doubt you are wondering the nature of the programme we are referring too."

"It began many years before the 2010 release of The Chase. The Skull & Bones Society, otherwise known as the Brotherhood of Death, the Order of the 322, had a dilemma.

"The powerful alumni behind the society pervaded the upper echelons of the American political and business arena. They had all come through the 'tapping' day' recruitment process at Yale University. However behind these primary members of the Order is a level of 'employees' who run the Order on a day-to-day basis. Clearly their recruitment cannot be carried out via traditional channels. It was becoming increasingly difficult to source people into these roles without drawing unwanted attention to the brotherhood."

"The idea was conceived to run a treasure hunt with a prize so irresistible thousands of everyday people would be drawn into its vortex. The progress of people through the hunt could be monitored, identifying individuals with the attributes desirable to be recruited into the Brotherhood."

"Forrest Fenn was approached early in the piece to create the treasure hunt. He had the skills and background to construct a puzzle so complex it would stretch even the cleverest minds. He was sufficiently remote from Yale to prevent folk from drawing a linkage between him and the Brotherhood."

"The hunt he created exceeded all expectations in its breadth and intricacy. It was built in such a way that there were no shortcuts to the end. Multiple levels had to be navigated and the outcomes pieced together to arrive at the conclusion. Even then there were numerous blind alleys and red herrings."

"Interestingly, Fenn included many of the aspects exclusive to the Order of 322 into the chase. In the opening Ouray hunt it includes the reference to Taps after the discovery of the Marble Cave, a nod to the crypt, the meeting hall of the Order on the Yale campus."

"Then there is the initiation ceremony for the inductees tapped to join the Order. It is a ritual cloaked in mystery, and only spoken of in hushed tones. Participants in the ceremony are sworn to secrecy and details of the goings-on have only leaked out occasionally over the

The Pearl Necklace

180-year history of the Society. Through the vague details known, it has been revealed the new recruits are blind folded at a remote location and then driven around New Haven to disorientate them. Eventually they are placed in a wooden coffin and transported to the crypt, still blind folded. There they are carried shoulder high into the crypt and placed on a stone stand in total darkness. Other members of the Order are present, surrounding the coffin and chanting over it. Eventually silence falls and the new recruitment relates there life history to the group. This can take hours, after which the inductee is removed from the coffin and stripped naked. They are then dressed in the garb of the Order with its insignia. Other rituals involving bones and a mud pile are then carried out into the early hours of the morning."

"At a date a few days later the ritual is repeated, with the inductee relating their sexual history in intimate detail. Is this why Fenn has included his own sexual history within the Chase? And has he exaggerated it to impress the members of the Order?"

"Earl, your families endeavour to uncover the secrets to the chase and discover the treasure are to be applauded. If any deserved to find the treasure it was you. There is however one fascinating aspect of the final solution you failed to pick up on. I'm sure you will find it intriguing."

"Like the Fibonacci sequence in the Da Vinci code, we have our very own Demosthenes sequence. We were surprised how you overlooked this connection in your book. Yes, our team of cyber hackers monitored with interest your year-long toil to put your adventures down onto paper."

"It is well-known by those familiar with the society that the 322 under the skull and cross bones in our emblem derives from the death date of Demosthenes in ancient Greece. But if the 322 was a sequence, what would the next digits be?

I knew the answer instantly and looked across at Colt. He raised his eyebrows at me to confirm we both had identified 111 as the correct response.

"We are not surprised you could solve this teaser in an instant. When designing the programme we calculated for someone, or a group, to solve the chase they would need the following:

- One or more individuals with an IQ over 140
- An intimate understanding of cryptic crosswords
- The talent for interpreting complex visual clues

E. Pairing

- The patience to spend hours on the internet researching endless clues
- The ability to recognise themes and patterns within mayhem, and piece them together
- The capacity to see themselves as the designer of the chase
- The drive and confidence to back their solution and venture into the wilderness
- The physical fitness to operate at 10,000 ft in the Rocky Mountains
- The skill and intellect to solve problems in real time in the great outdoors
- The perseverance to recover from repeated disappointment

"It would be extremely rare for all these attributes to be contained within a single person, and almost as rare to find it within a cohesive group. If you created a Venn diagram featuring all of these aspects, it would highlight the slim probability of one person, or team, having the complete package to solve the hunt and collect the treasure."

"Upon monitoring your group we quickly realised you had many of the bases covered within your team. Unfortunately though, there were other factors that precluded your entry into our inner circle."

"Earl, you drink far too much, and this leads to bad decisions, especially late at night. It may have contributed to you coming close to solving the chase but unfortunately makes you unsuitable for joining our exclusive team. And further to that, honestly, who would leave their only son to be eaten by a dangerous predator late at night anyway," quipped DB with a wide smile.

"We also eliminated Tyler and Briar-Rose early in the piece, as we are looking for unique individuals, and while they are a formidable duo, they are joined at the hip."

"And then we have Colt," said DB like a doting mother.

"I took the opportunity to interview him in the spa that night at St Elmo's Hotel. While quite stoned, he was still articulate and charming, a true gentleman, potentially making him a valuable addition to our team. After a further 12 months of observation, Bison Bill sealed the deal with him in the town park in Ridgway when you returned a year later."

"He has been working with us ever since, our boy wonder down under! In that time he has achieved some brilliant results, all of which

The Pearl Necklace

we can't divulge. And now he has convinced us to widen our recruitment programme globally."

"The Fenn Treasure Hunt has overall been a windfall for us. Over the 12 years we have had challenges, with the multiple fatalities, law suits, and death threats, but we have been able to navigate these successfully. We have managed to recruit a number of individuals who have now become key members of our organisation. Colt has convinced us replicating the recruitment exercise in your part of the world would produce even better results."

"We know you have been working on a treasure hunt of your own Earl, but have been hamstrung by a lack of funding to compile a treasure worthy of the effort. We are willing to help out with this small problem. In our possession we have a small golden frog, identical in every way to the original. It has been encased in a glass ball to be the centre piece of the newly created horde, sitting on a bed of pearls, as a tribute to Fenn's Hunt. Our backers feel a $AU 1M haul should be enough to garner the level of interest we are hoping to achieve."

"My god," I gasped, "this is a dream come true. My hunt has been sitting in the wings for so long awaiting its time. I would never compare it to Fenn's masterpiece as that would ridiculous. Believe me, it is intricate but designed to be solved. Fenn's chase was incredibly difficult. By comparison this is an 8 to his 10." I was struggling to find the right words, but like an over-excited school boy I carried on.

"I promise you there will be no riddles, and rest assured, sexual innuendo will not be the key to the securing the treasure."

"Finally there is one last surprise for you." DB declared enthusiastically, "Like I said at the beginning, this is the show that never ends!"

"To ensure absolute integrity of the solution, Fenn never revealed the final resting place of the treasure to us. However we do believe our own team has narrowed it down to a small area. The major clue is completing the Demosthenes sequence."

"Haven't we done that already," shot back Colt in a flash.

"Think about it a little longer," advised DB.

"OMG," Colt and I responded like identical twins.

"Four zeroes, how could we be so blind," Colt despaired, "3 22 111 0000."

3 22 111 0000

E. Pairing

"Blistering barnacles," I cried in my best Captain Haddock impression, "I get it now. One circle for each of the Castle Rocks – The Ouray delta, the Mt. Clayton Delta, Castle Rock Idaho, and finally the Outlet Colorado."

Leaping to my feet I grabbed a map of mainland USA from the already open map drawer. Laying it out on the desk, I carefully found each of the four Castle Rocks and marked a circle around them. By now Colt was up and pulling a long ruler from under the table. Placing it onto the map, he scribed a line from Idaho to the Outlet. He then moved the ruler slightly and repeated the process from Mt. Clayton to Ouray. As in all great treasure hunts, X marked the spot.

Pilot Butte, South Wyoming

No surprises there. It was perfectly in keeping with Fenn's sense of humour. The treasure was up Pilot Butte.

Colt was already on his phone. An online search showed Pilot Butte was the scene of a major event in 1885, known as the Rock Spring Massacre. It had been compared to the biblical destruction of Sodom and Gomorrah – razed to the earth due to its wickedness and crimes against nature, of anal and oral sex, and bestiality. The numerous cornhole references within Fenn's writings began to become clear.

"I don't think this is it" queried Colt. It is the good and evil thing again. Heaven and hell. Fenn is asking, am I a good man or an evil man? If I was a bad man I would be condemned to be buried here. I think the giveaway is the clue that led us here. It was all four nought. No man, no matter how evil, sees himself as a bad man. Surely Fenn would have wanted to the laid to rest in paradise."

"Yes, that's what we love about you Colt. You don't mind rocking the boat. You question everything and make up your own mind," beamed DB.

"This is all about the double Omega," continued Colt. "There are two possible routes to the treasure. One the virtuous route, with the three ones, leading us to the Garden of the Gods, where Fenn would provide directions to the chest. The second an evil route, with the 4 noughts leading us to hell on earth."

"Do we judge Forrest Fenn to be a good man, or a bad man?" came a voice from the darkness.

"Surely that is for God to decide," I responded.

"I don't feel The Finder found the treasure up Pilot Butte from the hints he has offered to date, but I do suspect Fenn wouldn't have created such an elaborate scheme without leaving something there, just like he did at the Ouray and Mt. Clayton delta's. Next time we are in the area I suggest we take a look up the butte and see what Fenn left behind."

"I'm picking it is a jar of pearls," shot out Colt.

On this occasion even DB rolled her eyes.

"It is only fitting Fenn's final resting place remains a mystery. There are many places within the search area that could be described as paradise. Hell, if you travel north from Pilot Butte the first place you come to is Eden. But no matter what, it is all academic as the treasure is no longer there."

"It is time to move on," said DB solemnly. "The Thrill of the Chase has served its purpose. We are satisfied it is time to close the curtains on it, and open a new chapter in the field of armchair treasure hunting."

"'The Hunt for the Golden Idol,' is the new holy grail. The Golden Frog trophy and $1M is there to entice a new generation of treasure hunters."

"Earl, how about you give us the starting clue from your hunt to whet our appetites," said DB invitingly.

"No worries," I replied, before pausing to take a long draw on my drink.

"Much like Fenn's masterpiece, my treasure hunt is based around a poem,19 verses in all. I can only hope it provides as much excitement and joy as the original chase. Here are the first two verses."

*I*t was a crazy moment, when it disappeared
        To resurface near the nine-pin gate
        Ride the fair highways of old Blackbeard
        Tis eventide for pieces of eight

*F*or I am using these shaky notes
        To guide you to the treasure trove
        Out of the blue, you see missing boats
        Moored inside long forgotten cove

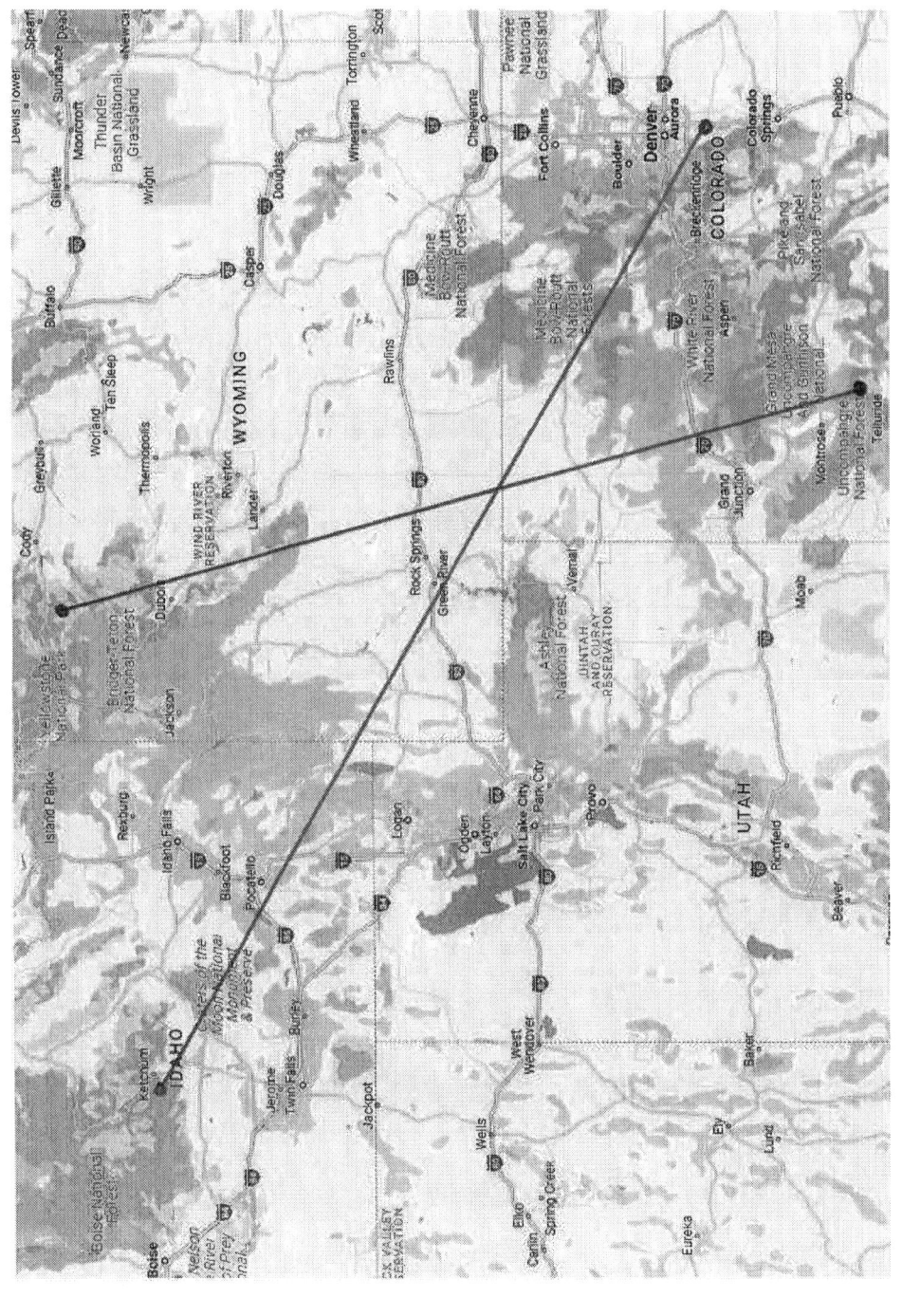

Made in United States
Troutdale, OR
10/23/2023